W9-BOC-253

Normal

Also by Lucia Nevai

Star Game: Stories
(Iowa Short Fiction Award Series)

Normal

stories by Lucia Nevai

Algonquin Books of Chapel Hill • 1997

Published by
ALGONQUIN BOOKS OF CHAPEL HILL
Post Office Box 2225
Chapel Hill, North Carolina 27515-2225

a division of
WORKMAN PUBLISHING
708 Broadway
New York, New York 10003

Printed in the United States of America.
Published simultaneously in Canada by Thomas Allen & Son Limited.
Design by Bonnie Campbell.

Some of the stories in this collection, many in different form, first appeared in other publications: "Close," *The New Yorker* (1988); "The Talking Woman," *American Fiction* (1992, no. 4); "The Good Luck Cake," *Gulf Coast* (1993); "Normal," *Not One of Us* (1993); "Belief," *No Roses* (1994); "Me, Gus," *Another Chicago Magazine* (1994); "Release," *Caprice* (1994); "The Drunk," *Iowa Review* (1995); "Monsieur Allé," *North Dakota Quarterly* (1995); "Thanksgiving with Dorrie & Heck," *Vignette* (1995); and "Silent Retreat," *North American Review* (1996).

Library of Congress Cataloging-in-Publication Data
Nevai, Lucia, 1945–
Normal : stories / by Lucia Nevai.
p. cm.
ISBN 1-56512-158-9 (hardcover)
I. Title.
PS3564.E848T48 1997
813'.54—dc21 96-47655
CIP

10 9 8 7 6 5 4 3 2 1
First Edition

Acknowledgments

I thank the wonderful editors who first published these stories in magazines and quarterlies: Dan Menaker, David Hamilton and Mary Hussmann, Sharon Solwitz, William Borden, Amy Storrow, Dawn Baille, James Mechem, Carolyn Koo, Richard Simon, John Benson, Michael White, Robley Wilson, Alan Davis.

I thank my exceptional agent, Michael Congdon, for his unique tenacity and unflagging conviction about the merits of my work.

I thank my editor, Marie Elizabeth Price, who opened the doors of Algonquin to this book and who carefully, creatively enhanced the details of these characters and their lives.

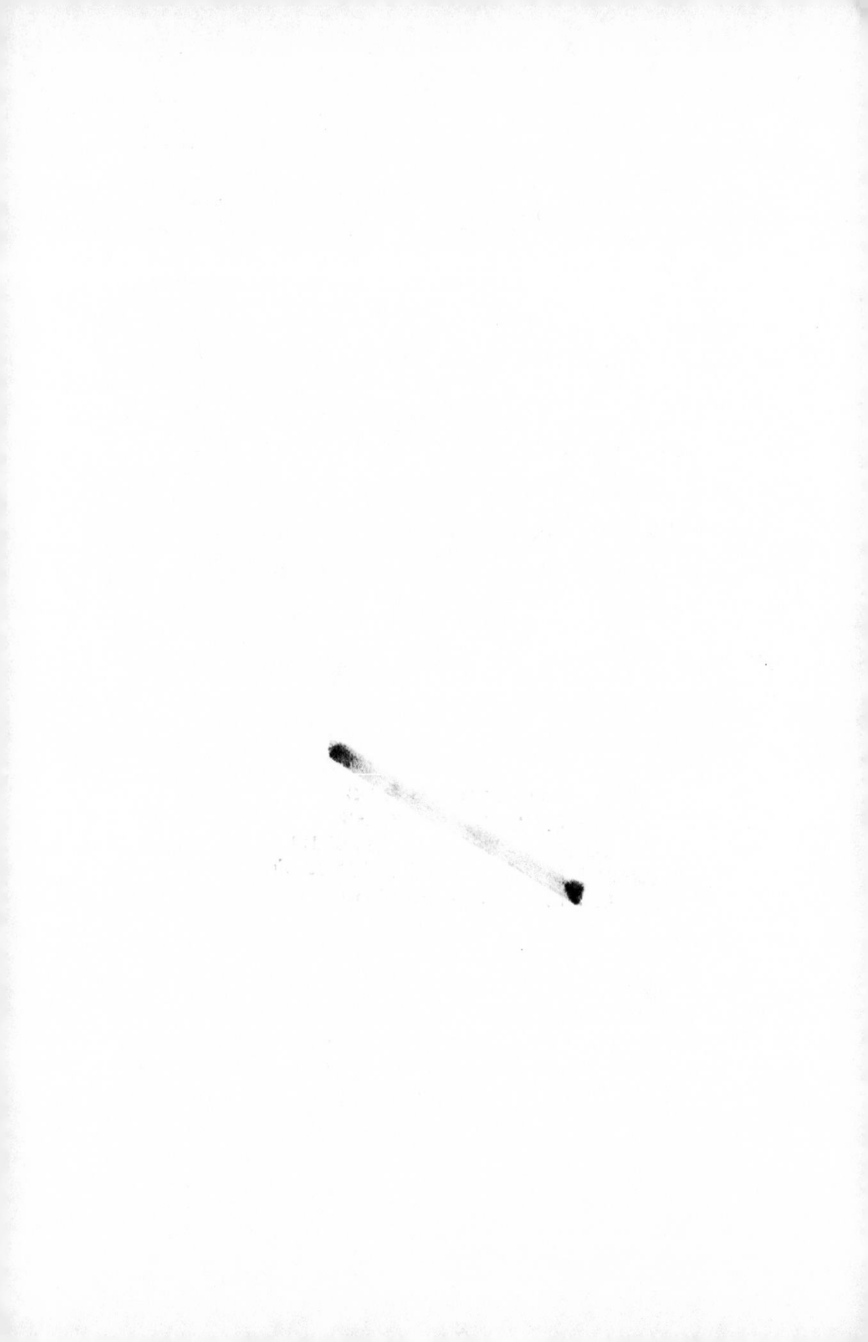

Contents

For my mother
who reads for the truth
and remembers it
to live by

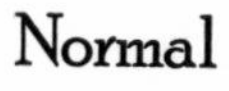
Normal

Part One

Monsieur Allé

Howie watched nervously as Glenda arranged his Crab and Ginger Egg Rolls on the stoneware platter. For color, she added a garnish of crisp, carved radish roses. Howie had shaved. He'd washed his hair—piles of wet curly silver hair fell over his forehead and ears. He'd put on a clean blue oxford cloth shirt. His shoulders were rounded from years of sitting hunched over at his desk writing wildlife documentaries. Howie was finally forty-five—his oversensitive morose expression had had the effect of making him look forty-five since nursery school. "Is there anything funny about this yet?" Howie asked.

"Not funny ha-ha," Glenda said. They sat down in the huge

leather Guatemalan club chairs and put their feet up on the matching ottomans. For the third time in as many weeks, they awaited Monsieur Allé, the child abuse investigator from the New York City Department of Special Services for Children.

Glenda's black cotton Chinese slippers peeked out from under the billowing yardage of a long batik dress, dyed with shades of purple and blue so enchanting, they managed to whisper of South Seas sunsets and turquoise oceans even here at Seventy-fourth and Broadway on the Upper West Side of Manhattan. At thirty-nine, Glenda's face was a collision of two centuries. Her girlhood beauty had embodied the nineteenth-century feminine ideals of hope, charity and mercy as portrayed in naive American statuary, but life had blasted her hot and hard and now the nerves of her face seemed too raw to feel hope, the smile too wary for charity, the huge green eyes too fearful of the absence of mercy everywhere to dispense their share. Her long, brown hair was thinning.

Glenda wondered why Monsieur Allé had originally seemed in such a big hurry to investigate Howie. He had wanted to come to the apartment within forty-eight hours of receiving the report of abuse from the Pierrepont School. Glenda was ruffled by his phone call—what to serve? Her signature appetizer, Warmed, Marinated Goat Cheese on Whole Wheat Cumin Pita Toasts, was passé. So she persuaded Howie to

make the crab rolls for Monsieur Allé. It crossed her mind that Monsieur Allé might take the appetizer as a bribe, an attempt to bolster a poor moral reputation with a rich culinary one, but she decided to proceed. Amazing appetizers were a family custom. To offer the Monsieur nothing, she reasoned, might add nuances of pretense and deceit to the investigation, casting an unwarranted shadow of suspicion.

Two dozen crispy, golden, delicate crab rolls were draining on paper towels that first night when Monsieur Allé had called from the bowels of Brooklyn, apologizing at length in his vaguely noble accent, saying that he could not keep the appointment because he was still in the process of investigating a family there. Glenda rescheduled. Howie wrapped and carefully froze the rolls.

They were sitting in the club chairs the next week with the crab rolls reheated and arranged on the platter, waiting for Monsieur Allé and listening to Classic Rock radio when the disc jockey broke the Every-Day-Is-a-No-Repeat-Day rule by playing Lynyrd Skynyrd's "Free Bird" twice in a row. Howie pulled Glenda up from the chair, and they twirled around on the area rug together in ecstasy, until a brutal shout from Roddy, Glenda's sixteen-year-old son, broke the mood.

"Phone!" he yelled, opening the door to his bedroom just wide enough to stick out his shaved head. Howie's nine-year-

old daughter, Mimi, was on the phone, calling from a booth at the corner of Ninety-sixth and Broadway. She was locked out of her mother's apartment—her mother was out of town on business and wouldn't be back until late. Howie took a cab up, let Mimi in with his key, then because Mimi was afraid to be alone, Howie called all three of the Allegras in Mimi's fourth grade class to try to arrange a spur-of-the-moment play date. No go. Howie brought Mimi home. The child abuse charge was a secret from her—how would he occupy her during Monsieur Allé's investigation?

When Monsieur Allé called to say in that lilting, vaguely aristocratic accent of his that he would be an hour late, Glenda explained in a whisper about the Mimi complication. Monsieur Allé respected this. The investigation was rescheduled for the following week.

Glenda wondered now if the initial jostling of the appointment time was contrived by Monsieur Allé to add to his information about the family. Perhaps the evaluation was already under way. As she looked about the room, wondering what he'd think of it, she felt sorry for her furnishings. The things she'd acquired over twenty years and three loves looked crowded and eccentric in this staid floor plan. Squeezed unsacredly onto the limited wall space were a pair of Tibetan Tangkas—complex, richly colored scrolls, symmetrically de-

signed for Buddhist meditation, though her first love, Sol, the father of Roddy, had used them more often as implements of seduction. The Guatemalan club chairs had somehow been toted north from Central America on a Volkswagen bug by Jean, father of Glenda's fourteen-year-old son, Neil. With Howie came the Mexican motif. Rustic wood chairs with high, straight backs and rush seats encircled a heavy, somber table. The set spilled out of the modest dining alcove like a fat man overflowing a folding chair. Glenda felt guilty, forcing things from three different men to mix within such conventional walls. Yet, considering all they'd been through, she was grateful her things had survived at all.

The bell rang at 7:15. Neil sprang to answer it. Tall and thin, wearing his customary black T-shirt and black jeans, Neil offered to take Monsieur Allé's tan detective coat. Some gold or brass totem of personal significance hung from a chain around Neil's neck. His dark-blond hair he wore in a ponytail that reached to the middle of his back. His face presented the same classic, even features as his mother's, but projected an elusive caginess and despair.

The mystery of the vaguely noble accent was revealed: Monsieur Allé was Haitian. His manner was gentle and dignified, his suit well made but not ostentatious, his eyeglasses round with gold wire frames. Glenda urged Monsieur Allé to

be seated on the sofa as near as possible to the appetizers. Roddy broke the embarrassing silence that ensued by crowing in a whining, theatrical English accent, "There was a bit of a nastiness last night, yes? Some very extreme nastiness, yes? A few of a certain Billy Boy's friends were ambulanced off, yes?"

Howie and Neil laughed heartily. Roddy had committed the entire dialogue of *A Clockwork Orange* to memory. Glenda studied the Monsieur's reaction to Roddy. He did not seem to be alarmed by Roddy's appearance. Good—she would not have to explain to him that although Roddy's head was shaved like a skinhead's, although he wore the same brand of heavy black lace-up boots skinheads wore and went to clubs where skinheads and longhairs broke each other's jaws, he went as a cultural observer, and was not, per se, a skinhead. Real skinheads were white supremacists. How could Roddy be a white supremacist when his father, Sol, was a child of the Holocaust? Roddy was serious, spiritually serious. The great blue dragon tattooed permanently on the full length of his arm proved it. Scarification was a male rite of passage; the dragon was a well-known symbol of spiritual evolution. It seemed obvious to Glenda that in a society which did not provide a sufficient ritual to mark a boy's transition into manhood, a serious youth made up his own. She had tried and failed to make up a transition ritual for Roddy—she'd dispensed with Chore Points.

Chore Points were allotted for voluntary chores, five points for Ajaxing the bathtub, three points for Windexing the kitchen cabinets, one point for Lemon-Pledging the coffee table. Chore Points could be amassed, then redeemed for Privileges: staying up late to watch TV, baking chocolate chip cookies with Mom even if Mom was tired, that kind of thing. Dispensing with Chore Points had failed to prepare Roddy for manhood. Glenda felt sorry—he was a male adrift in a psychotic culture with the millennium approaching like a tsunami.

Neil was also adrift, but unlike Roddy, he was not fascinated by people. He was misanthropic. He stayed in his room much of the time reading science fiction and *Guns & Ammo*. Both Neil and Roddy were brilliant. Nearly every teacher in the Pierrepont School had said so. Glenda had years of written evaluations confirming it. Over and over, the teachers would write, *Roddy* [or Neil] *shows no interest whatsoever in his homework, which is frustrating to me as both his test scores and his occasional in-class responses indicate he is brilliant.*

"These are Howie's special crab rolls," Glenda said to the Monsieur. We drink beer with them. Will you have one?"

Monsieur Allé did not drink alcohol, never had, he said, because in Haiti, he'd been a minister and wanted to set a good example. Now, in America, where standards were more lax,

it was too late for him to develop a taste for it. Tea was his drink, any kind of tea. Glenda brought him a pot of Lapsang Souchong.

Monsieur Allé opened his briefcase. "You are married?" he asked Howie, his pen poised over the first blank on the intimidating yellow investigation report.

"Yes," Howie said decisively. Less decisively he added, "To Mimi's mother."

"He doesn't want to hurt her feelings," Glenda explained.

"Plus, Glenda's still married to Neil's father," Howie pointed out.

"He doesn't believe in paying lawyers to achieve our emotional resolution," Glenda said.

"So Howie is your *boyfriend*," Monsieur Allé said to Glenda, neatly filling in the blank. He moved his pen down a line. "Roddy and Neil are whose sons?"

"Different people's," Glenda said. She explained about Sol and Jean.

"They live here full time?" Monsieur Allé asked.

"We are all here full time," Glenda said. "Howie and I make sure that one or both of us are here every day when the boys get out of school."

Monsieur Allé's dark eyes darted from Roddy and Neil to Glenda and Howie. "Why?"

"We just want to be here for them," Glenda said. "To make up for no one being there for them when they were little. If they want to ask for my help on homework or get Howie's advice on girls, we're here."

Monsieur Allé's brow was furrowed in bafflement. "And do they ask for your help on homework?"

"No," Glenda said. "They come home stoned and go straight to their rooms and listen to loud, robotic, post-punk nihilistic German bands. You should hear this awful music, Monsieur Allé."

"And do they ask your advice on girls, Howie?" Monsieur Allé asked.

"No. But I think it's important that I'm here. They're growing up with a creative male in the home."

"Your daughter," Monsieur Allé said. "She doesn't need to grow up with a creative male in the home?"

"No, she needs a breadwinning female, who's capable, flexible, bright, beautiful and never is home," Howie said.

Monsieur Allé's eyes darkened expressively, his shoulders stiffened. He returned to the investigation report. "Neil, please summarize the incident that occurred three weeks ago."

"Howie. Was in the kitchen. Making spicy. Oven-fried chicken." Neil respectfully spoke at the pace that Monsieur Allé was capable of writing script.

Glenda watched the Monsieur's pen as it formed lines of even, flowing lowercase letters. "Look, Howie," she said. "If our kids had gone to public school in Haiti instead of going to private progressive school in Manhattan, they would be able to write traditional script instead of printing everything in that unpredictable mixture of capital and lowercase letters."

Monsieur Allé read the sentence back to Neil, making it a question. "*Howie* was in the kitchen making Spicy Oven-fried Chicken?"

"It was Howie's night to cook," she said, interrupting. "We have an equal opportunity kitchen. Howie made these." She explained how the crab rolls were made and listed the twenty-two ingredients. "Try one."

"I was in the middle of something," Neil said with annoyance.

"Continue," Monsieur Allé said, eschewing the crab rolls.

"I came in. To get. Some potato chips. Howie was taking pieces. Of raw chicken. Out of the package. And rolling them. In flour."

"That's called *dredging*," Glenda said to Neil.

"Howie was dredging. I said to Howie. Did you wash. The chicken first. He beat me up."

Monsieur Allé's eyes grew dark and thunderous. He was impressed. "Who witnessed this?" he asked. Glenda raised her hand.

Roddy half-raised his, saying, "I came in for the ball-kicking."

"Ball-kicking," Monsieur Allé echoed. "My, my."

"We lived in a commune in Vermont," Glenda blurted out. "There was no authority figure. Everyone raised everyone. We ate organically grown food. The apricots got mealy worms. There were bugs in the whole wheat flour. We got lice. It wasn't the future. It was the past, the past that progress had improved. I left Jean." Everyone was staring at Glenda.

"Howie," Monsieur Allé said. "What is your side?"

"It's true," Howie said. "I *was* making Spicy Oven-fried Chicken. I coat the chicken with a special mixture of flour, salt and pepper, paprika, cayenne pepper, garlic powder and toasted sesame seeds."

"Sesame seeds," Monsieur Allé said, his eyes shining with a special Caribbean brightness.

"You toast them first," Howie said. "Mimi was having dinner with us. Spicy Oven-fried Chicken is her favorite dish. I was also making mashed potatoes—Neil will only eat potato products, mashed potatoes, french fries, potato knishes, potato chips. And I was making Green Beans in Olive Oil with garlic for Roddy. Because he's avoiding meat for ninety days as a purge. He'd been through a raw phase. He read a book about the precious enzymes and healthful minerals in raw foods. He ate a lot of raw oysters and steak tartar. Apparently

for some people these are the keys to longevity. They made him sick."

Everyone relaxed while Monsieur Allé wrote down the menu and its rationale. The boys dipped the crab rolls in the sauce. Howie ate the radish roses. Glenda drank two Tsing-Tao beers. Monsieur Allé, she observed, would be well served by a tape recorder. "Continue," Monsieur Allé said.

"So Neil is walking back and forth in front of me," Howie said. "Eating potato chips. Watching me. And making a face."

"What kind of face?"

Howie demonstrated, bloating his face slightly in the cheeks, mouth and jaw, as if he were two seconds away from vomiting. Neil looked proud of himself.

"That face. Seven years I've been cooking for him and what do I get. Always that face. He stands there eating the chips, watching me, making that face. Then he says, Did you wash the chicken first. I stop what I'm doing. It's important to wash the chicken first, he says, to remove the grody slime. Look, dickhead, I say, the chicken is not for you. The potatoes are for you. And I point him to the pot on the range where the potatoes are boiling. If I have time, I make real mashed potatoes. If not, I buy Idahoan. Idahoan are the only instant dehydrated potatoes that taste like homemade." When Monsieur Allé had caught up, Howie went on.

"So, Neil goes to the pot, he lifts off the cover, he looks inside. He's still making that face. Say one word and you're dead, I say to him. Ugh, he says. I have this nice fat floury chicken thigh in my hand. And something comes over me, and I throw it at him. It hits him hard right in his face—smack! There's a little puff of flour in the air like gunpowder. The thigh falls to the floor. He picks up the thigh and throws it back at me. It hits me here in the chest. Pow, I get him in the face. Pow, in the neck. As fast as I can throw them at him, that's how fast he's throwing them back."

Monsieur Allé had stopped writing and was listening with an arrested expression. Glenda crossed her legs daintily at the ankle. "You've got a good home here," Roddy quoted to Neil in his whining English accent, "good loving parents. You've got not too bad of a brain. Is it some devil that comes inside of you?" Neil was laughing soundlessly.

"There was flour everywhere," Howie said. "Flour all over me, all over Neil, all over the floor, the table, the chairs. Everywhere. Mimi happens to walk into the room to ask a question about her history chapter."

"She's very bright," Glenda said.

"I say, Not now, Mimi. We're ducking, we're kicking over chairs, chicken is flying. Mimi screams at me to help her with her history chapter. I say, For God's sake, Mimi, not now. She

runs out of the apartment and runs twenty blocks up Broadway to her home, only her mother's out of town on business and Mimi's forgotten her key, so she has to come back."

"You witnessed this," Monsieur Allé said, turning a suspicious eye on Glenda.

"We lived in a tepee on Mount Shasta one summer," Glenda said. "We had a goat. We carried water from a spring."

"We're down to a few raw chicken backs," Howie said. "I get him hard in the cheek. It smarts—I can see that. So I say, Let's call it quits. Fuck you, he says, and fuck your mother where she breathes. Don't ever say that about my mother, I say, now go to your room. He won't go. I attempt to bodily remove him from the kitchen. He kicks me in the balls."

"A shock," Roddy whined, "sending my dada beating his bruised and krowy lukkers and unfair Bog in his heaven and my mom boo-hooing in her mother's grief about her only son letting everybody down real horrorshow."

"I grab him," Howie said. "By the skin on his back. And push him out of the apartment and into the hall. When you're prepared to apologize for what you said about my mother, you can come back, I said.

"Did he apologize?" Monsieur Allé asked.

"She let him in," Howie said, pointing to Glenda.

"Howie told me to," she said.

"How long was he out there?"

Howie and Glenda looked at each other, trying to remember precisely. "It's hard to judge the passage of time in a family crisis," Glenda said. "A minute seems like an hour and an hour seems like a minute."

"Ten minutes," Roddy said crisply. "Howie locked the door at 7:50 and unlocked it so Neil could see *The Cosby Show*."

"Did he apologize?" Monsieur Allé demanded. Neither Howie nor Glenda could remember. Monsieur Allé seemed disappointed.

"Jean's mother always washed the chicken," Glenda said.

Monsieur Allé consulted the official complaint form in his file. "There were bruises," he said.

"I saw the bruises when I went in to say goodnight to Neil," Glenda said. "He had his shirt off and was looking at the bruises in the mirror. There were terrible marks on his back, on the shoulder blades and the upper spine where Howie grabbed him. I went to get ice packs, but Neil wouldn't let me back in his room. He didn't want me anywhere near him, did you, Neil?"

Glenda watched Neil shrink even now at the thought of her barging in with her leaky, ice-cube-filled baggies.

"How did the bruises on your back come to the attention of Ms. Lambert-Castor?" Monsieur Allé asked Neil, reading from the complaint form. Neil drew a blank.

"He means Cynthia," Glenda said to Neil. To Monsieur Allé, she said, "Everyone at the Pierrepont School, even the head, is on a first-name basis."

"I told my friend that Howie beat me up," Neil said. "He told Cynthia."

"Five years I helped her with the silent auction," Howie said to Monsieur Allé. "I called parents. I picked up donations. I set up tables."

"She *is* legally bound as a school official to call it in," Monsieur Allé stated.

"Five years," Howie said. "Watch her call me again this fall. "No more. Comprende, señor? No más."

"It's an anti-parent school," Glenda explained. "We purposely picked it because we didn't want to impose our values on our kids. We wanted Roddy and Neil to individuate, even if it meant hating us a little earlier than they normally would. And you did, didn't you, boys?"

Monsieur Allé had not written anything down since the first piece of chicken was thrown. He was sipping his tea, and looking at Glenda with pity and contempt.

"Roddy and Neil," he said eventually, "Did Howie ever

throw things at you before, did he ever strike you?" The boys laughed.

"My problem's passivity," Howie admitted.

"It works for me, babe," Glenda said. She and Howie clasped hands.

"Oh God, here they go," Neil said to Roddy.

"Why don't you two do the frug for Monsieur Allé," Roddy said to Glenda and Howie. "A-one, a-two." He snapped his fingers in time as Neil sang the opening guitar riff of Jimi Hendrix's cover of "All Along the Watchtower."

"We're secure enough in our relationship to let them tease us," Glenda instructed the Monsieur.

"So Howie has never treated the boys in a way that frightened them?" Monsieur Allé said, sticking to the point.

"Put it this way," Glenda said. "The day I told him he'd been reported by the Pierrepont School for child abuse was shopping day. He was very upset when he shopped. What's this, I said, when I unpacked. He'd bought Pepperidge Farm Milanos. Neil likes *Mint* Milanos. After what Neil did to me, Howie said, he's not getting Mint Milanos. He's getting regular."

Monsieur Allé was frowning deeply. He refilled his cup from the teapot. He sipped. He continued as if by rote. "Glenda, did you ever throw things at the boys or strike them?"

"I threw plates at Jean twice," Glenda admitted. "I once

grabbed Roddy hard by the upper arms. He had marks on his skin. When you were three," she said to Roddy.

"So, no one is or was in the habit of striking you?" Monsieur Allé asked the boys.

Neil raised his chin provocatively as if to take one on it right then and there. Roddy drummed on his thigh with the flats of his hands, a fast, frenetic polyrhythm. Glenda was remembering the last big horrible fight the boys had had with Jean. "No," Neil said finally, shaking his head with annoyance. "They have a good relationship with Jean," Howie volunteered in a voice as bright and persuasive as a game show host's. "They go to Vermont every summer. Well, they used to before—. They're city kids now. And Sol is—."

"We don't know where Sol is," Roddy said curtly.

A demoralized silence filled the room. An impression of the underlying brutality of family life seized Glenda. The furnishings in the room shimmered with years of rage and pain, deadly, dull, throbbing, unresolvable. Errors in judgment, lapses in thinking issued with a sour insistence as palpable as heat waves from Glenda's things. "Goats are a lot of work," she said shrilly. "You have to milk them twice a day. Goat's milk is too strong to drink, but the cheese is wonderful. We had goat cheese twenty years before it showed up on every menu in Manhattan."

Religious generosity overtook Monsieur Allé's professional disgust with Glenda and Howie. His eyes shone with grace. "You are nice people," he said quietly. He folded the official complaint form and the yellow investigation report in half, then in quarters. He was legally required, he explained, to detain the children privately and invite them to add to their statements without the parents being present.

Glenda and Howie withdrew to the kitchen. She called Avi's, the healthy neighborhood pizzeria, and ordered an extra-large pie with mushrooms and green peppers on one half, spinach and garlic on the other and extra cheese over the whole. The garlic was for Roddy, the green peppers for Neil, the mushrooms for Howie and the garlic for herself. Mixing up the halves like that and adding extra cheese drove up the price of the pie to thirty-seven dollars, but Glenda believed anything so simple that made everyone happy was worth the cost.

She peeked into the living room a few times as the boys continued with Monsieur Allé. She couldn't catch specific words or phrases, but based on their arm movements and gestures, they were taking turns describing the tepee, the fire where they cooked, the goat pen they built, the brook they walked to for water. Monsieur Allé looked homesick.

He rose from the sofa, briefcase in hand. Neil went to the

closet to retrieve the Monsieur's detective coat. Glenda and Howie came forth from the kitchen to see him to the door. While they were waiting for the elevator, Monsieur Allé got to talking with Howie about Haiti. He felt guilty, leaving his congregation in Port-au-Prince without a minister, but he had to flee that regime to give his wife and six children a chance for a better life.

"Six children!" Howie said to Glenda. "Think of the tuition bills if they all went to the Pierrepont School."

"What are their names?" Glenda asked, expecting a litany of powerful, vowel-heavy Afro-Caribbean syllables, but Monsieur Allé and his wife had chosen All-American New Testament names. As he uttered them, the light in his eyes reflected the special nature of each. They were serious, sly, weak, strong, gentle and playful. He was strict with them—he explained the details. There were curfews, minimum acceptable report cards, duties to complete at home. Serious spankings were the consequence of nonperformance.

Howie was spellbound. The elevator came and went twice as Howie continued to ask Monsieur Allé to give examples of infractions, swearing, failing a test, forgetting to do the laundry. They talked so long the pizza came.

It smelled delectable and spicy, so delectable and spicy, Glenda couldn't blame the boys for opening the box right in

front of Monsieur Allé, though that forced her, given her standards of politeness, to offer him some.

"Won't you stay for a slice, Monsieur Allé?" she said.

He looked hungrily at the delicious sizzling pie. He really should be getting home, he said. "Please stay," she said. His wife always kept his dinner warm, he said. His nose got a wrinkle in it when he said *dinner*, as if he'd smelled chlorine. Glenda understood—his wife, though fertile, was not a good cook. "It's our custom that you stay," she said, grabbing his briefcase out of his hand. They seated themselves at the huge somber table and ate the pie and while they ate, Howie asked Monsieur Allé to tell again about how he spanked his sons.

The Good Luck Cake

Ardor got off the propane gas truck at the north end of the town of Plaquemine, Louisiana. He thanked the driver for the ride and limped toward the Mississippi River with his cane, dragging the left leg. His strawberry-gray hair was combed back from his forehead in oily ridges that held the imprint of the comb. His face looked combed too. The skin lay in folds on his forehead and under the eyes; the folds fanned out like parentheses around the corners of the mouth. He was old, but not wise.

The truck had bad shocks. He'd ridden straight through from the Veterans Home in Houma. The concussion of the ride still echoed in his leg bones. All his energy went into the

leg. It had been shattered in World War II. The Army doctors had pieced it together with metal plates, pins, pegs—whatever they had handy. Every day since then, the hardware hurt. He was nothing but a limp.

Ardor stopped in front of his sister's cottage. When she first married, he'd visited her here. Her cottage backed right up to the Mississippi River then. Now, there was a wall of grass, the levee, blocking the river from view. And the tree was gone. The cypress in the side yard. All that was left of it was a stump five feet in diameter. Ardor hated it when they left a tree like that. It looked castrated. Better to go to the extra trouble of bulldozing the whole root ball out of the ground, to forget the tree and the shade it made, so you weren't left thinking about the way things used to be.

A girl skipped up as if she were expecting him. "This is my square-dance skirt," she announced. She twirled around a few times. The skirt spun straight out, revealing plump legs in patterned tights. Her long blue-black hair spun out like the skirt. She stopped twirling. Her face was shaped like a valentine; her skin was the English bone white. Her eyes were a cool wolf blue. She folded her arms across her chest, hiding promising tweaks of breasts. "You are Ellie's brother from Houma, aren't you, sir," she said with respect. The familiarity Ardor could have predicted; the respect caught him off guard.

"I am," he said. "And you are?"

"Freda Perret. I added on to Ellie's letters."

Ardor wondered what Freda Perret had been writing to him. The last few years, he'd been throwing away his sister's letters without reading them. They were all the same and they made him feel bad. They began with a list of which flowering trees were in bloom, continued with joyous descriptions of miracles of abstinence occurring in the parish and concluded with love and forgiveness for his withdrawal, silence and bitterness. Women could sit in their kitchens and believe anything they wanted. What they believed didn't apply. "How do you do," he said, leaning on his good leg and shaking her hand.

"Just fine, thank you." Freda was giving him a significant look. Some reaction on his part was required.

"Why are you looking at me like that?" he asked.

"I expect you *forgot*, sir," Freda said. Her manner was nurse-like, testing his faculties.

"Forgot what?"

Freda was pleased. Her features grew luminous with sympathy, which had the effect of making her seem to move closer. "It's the amnesia, isn't it," she said, her voice lowered confidentially—the sacred word was safe with her. What romantic war tales had Ardor's sister told this little neighbor girl?

"What'd I forget?"

Freda took his hand in both of hers. She coached him. "Ellie's daughter, Dolly, your niece, found a nice, clean Catholic nursing home for Ellie in Baton Rouge last year. On account of the two falls she had."

"Oh, no." His voice was a croak far back in his throat. He'd bummed the ride with the gas man today to ask for four hundred dollars. He'd lost it over the past few months playing cards. He couldn't go back to Houma without it. His throat would be slit in the middle of the night by the lunatic in the wheelchair with the eight-inch bowie knife.

Ardor stared at the white, square cottage. It shimmered in the heat, threatening to disappear altogether. He needed a small miracle, the kind his sister was constantly reporting as the direct result of the prayers of the people around here.

"Ellie prayed you'd visit," Freda said. "I told her you would. I told her if she prayed that hard, you would. She had nothing but faith in you. She defended you constantly to your other sister."

"My other sister." Ardor had forgotten about her. He wondered if she could be squeezed for the four hundred. "Where is she living now?"

"On Bayou Teche."

Still on Bayou Teche—she couldn't be squeezed. "Who

lives here now?" Ardor asked. Somebody owed him something.

"A boy named Kenwood," Freda said. "And his younger brother, Robert, who's my age. Robert knows all about you. He constantly asks me to tell him about all you did for us in France."

Ardor leaned hard on the cane. His bones hurt. He had four hours to kill until the gas man came back through. He needed a couple of dollars for a drink. He wondered if this girl had any allowance saved up.

"You're looking peaked, sir," she said. "Would you like a cold drink?"

Ardor followed her across the road to her house. She skipped ahead, then ran back to walk with him at his agonizingly slow pace. "My mother is up the street, decorating the church. There's a farewell party this evening for a boy named Mark. He's in the Army. He's going to the Middle East. My mother spent three and a half hours making the frosting."

The kitchen was dark and cool. "Sit anywhere," she said. He picked a chair with its back to the wall, and straightened out his bad leg to give the knee a rest.

Freda poured him a glass of iced tea. She stood close to him, her knees touching his good knee, watching him drink. He drank with disappointment—tea was tea. His eyes swept the

cabinets over the refrigerator and the range—good places for liquor to be kept.

As if she could read his mind, she said, "How are you doing with *it all*, sir?" *It all* was how Ellie used to refer to his drinking problem.

"Not well," he admitted.

"Don't you worry about it," she said. Her voice caught him up like a safety net, a sudden overall touch. She was so close and her eyes were so blue. He felt a pang: if only he had a girl to talk to now and then.

He smiled. "You're kind," he said.

"I have a weight problem," she confided. She moved to his side, resting a hand on his shoulder. "My boyfriend told me if I don't go to Weight Watchers, he's going to stop being my boyfriend and start being my cousin's boyfriend. Isn't that mean? He's in a wheelchair. He's got a muscular disease. I would never expect a person in a wheelchair to be mean, would you?"

"The meanest ones are the ones in chairs," Ardor said. He felt sorry for himself. The lunatic at the Veterans Home would oil up the chair so it didn't squeak, roll in to Ardor's room and slash him. Maybe it was time somebody finished off what they started in France. Maybe it was the same problem as the tree —now it was nothing but a big, disappointing stump in place of a beautiful, shady, silver cypress. Instead of getting rid of

the whole thing, roots and all, so people could think about something new, the stump sat there, a glaring reminder of what used to be.

"We had an intruder," Freda said. "Two weeks ago Tuesday. Looking in the bathroom window at my mother while she took a bath. She called Robert's father—." In deference to Ardor's possible amnesia, she explained again. "Robert is the boy that lives in Ellie's house now. And Robert's father came over here with a shotgun. The man ran down the levee. That kind of thing has never before happened in Plaquemine. Now, my mother locks the door at night and instead of leaving her grocery money on the table here, she hides it in that vase."

Ardor cheered up. It was a blue-green vase, very classical and female in shape. It sat on the counter next to the wall phone. He sensed the presence of bills inside, soft, woven, genuine U.S. Treasury notes.

"Would you like to see the cake?" she asked.

"What cake?"

"The cake my mother made for Mark, the boy who's going to the Middle East." On the table was a rectangular cake pan covered with aluminum foil. Freda pried up the edges of the foil with care. "You should have seen the vomitty colors she threw out before she came up with these. She borrowed a pair of shorts from Robert to copy the pattern."

She lifted off the foil.

Ardor leaned forward to look. The cake was a terrible mistake. It was frosted to look like camouflage: awful amoeba-like shapes in three awful shades of olive drab. Even worse, the words GOOD LUCK were written in white frosting on top of the awful green. Ardor grimaced and twisted away. "I wouldn't show the boy that."

Freda's features grew crisp, her voice crisper. "It took her nearly a day to make it. Three and a half hours on the frosting alone. She threw out one whole batch and started over to get it right." She replaced the foil cover indignantly.

They could sit in their kitchens and believe anything they wanted. "Where's the lavatory?" he said.

She pointed to the door off the kitchen. Ardor organized himself to stand up, crooking the bad leg at the knee, pushing himself away from the wall to get up the momentum to rise. Someone knocked at the screen door, a little black boy. Freda ran outside. "Robert," she said, "guess who's here? Mr. Ardor Landy. He came to visit Ellie. He's having a flashback. You just missed it."

Ardor used the toilet, washed his face and hands, brushed his teeth with someone's blue toothbrush, combed his oily hair with someone's black comb. He lit a cigarette and smoked it, leaning against the window frame, looking out at the still, stagnant water of the bayou.

Thirty years ago when he was here, the bayou was busy with river traffic, barges, trawlers, small fishing vessels. They came to Plaquemine from serious distances on inland waterways; all were heading for New Orleans. It was something to see, the way they lined up and waited for a turn in the deep, iron coffin of the lock. The rising water lifted them up. Boom, they were released into the high, wide brightness of the Mississippi. Ellie's husband had come to Plaquemine to operate the lock. That was the kind of job Ardor understood. There were big wheels, interlocking gears, great iron gates, loud whistles. There was a system, based on mechanics. No wonder they'd been a happy couple.

Now, the lock was closed. The levee blocked access to the Mississippi. The bayou ended boom, like that, in a forty-foot-high wall of grass. It was the way things ended in nightmares, bridges emptied into steel cages, stairs rose into thin air. They should have done it differently, so you weren't left thinking about the way it used to be. It was the same problem as the cypress tree.

Ardor leaned his forehead against the windowpane, then pulled back distastefully, remembering the intruder. This had to be the window. He flicked the cigarette butt into the toilet bowl and dragged his bad leg out of the room without flushing. He groped along the wall into the kitchen and paused at the vase.

Freda was standing outside, her back to the screen door, talking to Robert. "He made a face like this when he saw the cake," she was saying. " 'I wouldn't show the boy *that*,' he said."

Ardor stuck his hand inside the vase. It was a small wad, ones mostly, a wrinkled five, a twenty, more than enough for a couple of drinks. He slipped the stash into his pocket—they shouldn't be looking at things with rose-colored glasses, these women—then limped to the door to be introduced to Robert. It wasn't every day a boy got to meet a hero.

The Talking Woman

The Grand Canyon was a high-concept environment. Three hundred miles long, nine miles wide and a mile deep, it could be seen from space, cutting across Arizona like a scar. Vic was seeing it from the bottom. He was white-water rafting down the Colorado River. A client of his at home in Ann Arbor, Michigan, had done the eight-day white-water rafting adventure and recommended it. Vic only had time for the one-day—he was in the Southwest on business. The client had met people from all over the world on the raft. Strange things happened. He himself had a fit of anger one night for no reason, went off by himself and burst into tears: the faces of all the people he'd ever loved passed before him.

Vic was not mentally comfortable with the raft. It was a fourteen-foot-long oval canvas inner tube mounted on fiberglass pontoons. The bulky Day-Glo life vest he wore kept snagging his underarm hair. It made him feel bloated and slightly comical like that cartoon man made of tires. The benches where the passengers sat were hard and crowded. An aluminum safety rail ran along the inside of the inner tube, but it was hot to the touch. It was only 10 A.M. and the captain had just announced the temperature as 105. The sheer cliffs of the inner gorge blocked most of the canyon from view. Heat, miles of dry, scorching desert heat funneled down onto Vic's head—wasn't heat supposed to rise?

As the raft glided slowly along in the glassy water, Vic had to fight to recognize himself. In heat like this, he didn't sweat, he melted. It felt like the time he took the wrong drug and everyone else was having a wild time. He had to work assiduously for hours to avoid disintegrating; his surface kept threatening to separate like a slinky into a wobbly wire spiral with nothing inside.

Since early this morning, a passenger had been bothering him, a large, middle-aged woman with exhausted peroxide hair and mushy, red features. Hard as it was to negotiate the transfer from one end of the raft to the other, the woman

managed to follow Vic whenever he tried to elude her. She insisted on conversing with him nonstop, even when he didn't converse back. Vic was uncommunicative by nature. He could sing and when he did—he performed on weekends in a Lite Rock band in University of Michigan bars—things came out the way he meant them. At work, he did a lot of talking, a lot of motivating. He had a very good job in sales management—he'd worked his way to the top. But it wasn't communicating. It was more like giving blood. Whatever it drained away was so essential he could only replace it on weekends through solitude and singing.

Vic managed to escape the obnoxious woman passenger now, squeezing his way back to the rear bench. He sat down next to the captain, a Hualapai Indian whose Anglo name, as he put it, was Tom. "Like the way you run the river," Vic said.

Tom looked straight ahead. A black felt cowboy hat shaded his eyes. His hair was long and straight, gathered at the nape in a tooled silver clasp. He wore blue jeans and a Grateful Dead T-shirt. "I just watch her and listen," Tom said. "River tells me what to do. After twelve years, she and me get along just fine."

"Feels that way," Vic said.

Kathy, the first mate, was passing out snacks. She was a

tomboy, tiny and athletic. “How long has Kathy been doing it?” Vic asked, getting personal. Kathy was Tom’s girlfriend.

Tom looked at Vic hard. “Two years she’s been with me,” he said with an undertone of blame as if he were still angry at another woman for leaving him.

“You work well together,” Vic said.

“I ain’t one for discussions.”

Vic smiled. He wasn’t either, but he couldn’t get away with it in his line of work. He envied the way Tom raised a hand or nodded his chin and Kathy knew which task he wanted done. Tom signaled Kathy now. She put away the snacks. He shut off the outboard. She dropped anchor. With the raft stationary at the bottom of the canyon, sitting close to Tom, Vic felt momentarily secure.

“Okay, people,” Tom said. He took off his hat and held the brim with both hands like an old-fashioned suitor. “Geology lesson.”

The passengers turned on their benches to face Tom. They were a fairly savvy group and, as Vic’s client predicted, from all over: three French medical students, two men and a woman; an elderly German-speaking couple; a young Australian mountaineer. The rest were single women, a group who worked for the same corporation. The annoying talker spotted Vic and clambered over the benches to get to him. She

held a Coors Light in one hand, a thin brown ladies' cigarette in the other. She squeezed down by Vic, talking about the time she lost her Bic lighter in Yellowstone National Park.

Tom waited for her to finish, then when she didn't, he gave Kathy a sign, wheeling a finger in front of his lips: stop the blabbermouth. Kathy placed both hands on the woman's shoulders in a teacherly fashion. "No talking when Tom is talking."

"Oh my God, am I talking?" the woman said. "Is he talking? I'll shut up. I'm sorry. I didn't hear him talking."

There were derisive titters among the passengers. The talking woman basked in the attention. She mimed locking her mouth shut and throwing away the key. Coors and cigarette still in hand, she made a halo over her head. Vic was certain his client had not had to deal with anything like this.

"Okay," Tom said. "Everybody see that there first layer?" Tom pointed to a dull charcoal-colored stripe at water level. Until Tom said *layer*, Vic had completely missed the striped character of the inner gorge. Something so obvious, and for the past three hours it had escaped him. "That black there," Tom said, "we call Vishnu schist, okay? Vishnu schist is lava laid down two billion years ago."

"That's how long it feels like since I laid down," the German said in a little toy Arnold Schwarzenegger accent. The passen-

gers laughed. The sound of laughter set the talking woman off: she talked about being one of six children, the only girl. Her brothers constantly played pranks on her, tripping her, teasing her, making a fool of her. Repeated shushings from Kathy only caused the woman to lower her volume. Tom talked over her voice. Vic, who wasn't that strong in geology to begin with, strained to follow Tom's lesson.

"After your lava layer," Tom said, "next thing that happens, thousands of years go by. Seas invade the area. Then, they dry up. Leave behind sediment. That there white layer above the black—everybody see that? That's your sediment."

The talking woman sang, "Go-in on a sed-i-men-tal journey." No one laughed. "You don't know that song?" she asked the group. Kathy shushed her. "You're all too young," she whispered.

"Next layer is your sandstone layer," Tom resumed. "Sandstone comes from sand. Your winds create your sculpting effect. Then, you get upthrust. Forces in the earth. Same kind of upthrust that produced your Rockies, your Andes, your Himalayas. Everything moves up. Reason why this here stayed like this for two billion years is no rainfall. Okay? If the Grand Canyon had tried to form in Maryland, it would be a small mound covered with trees."

Huh? Vic thought.

Tom yanked the outboard alive. The raft crept slowly forward. Vic asked Tom to explain. "It's like this," Tom said. "Nature makes a pencil line. Then nature erases it. Each generation of men sees one pencil line. But here in the canyon, we get to see all the pencil lines on display, one on top of the other."

Tom seemed consoled by this. Vic wanted to learn how to feel this way from Tom. He admired Tom. Tom was at home and adept in a hostile place. Tom knew the Colorado, where it was shallow, where it was deep, where the rocks were treacherous, where the springs were warm enough to swim. What did Vic know? Numbers. As head of Regional Consumer Sales for International Cookie, he knew quotas filled for the quarter, percent increases over last year's total. *Hike to the Top of Munchies Mountain*. That was the theme Vic chose for this year's incentive plan. There was the Triscuit Trail, the Premium Saltines Pass, the Oreo Overlook. Inching past the two-billion-year-old stone, Vic felt dispensable. Tom signaled Kathy. She sprang into action, passing out soda, sparkling water, juice.

"Got any beer in there?" the talking woman asked, as if it were her first of the day. It wasn't—she'd been drinking since 8 A.M. "Gimme one. What the hell, gimme two, save you the trouble." Kathy handed her the cans. "It's happy hour some-

where in the world," she said, just as Vic feared she would. He moved away, up to the middle bench.

Vic was exhausted. He had not slept well. The air conditioner in the motel room was loud and inadequate. From the beginning, during his long drive, Vic had not had good feelings about that motel. He could see it for half an hour before he reached it, floating like a mirage in the middle of the desert. The closer he got, the more surreal it seemed, a row of narrow rooms with numbered orange doors. Mammoth parking places were painted on the concrete strip in front of each door. It looked like a life-size board game designed by an existentialist, the kind of thing where the motel doors simply opened on more desert.

The girl who had checked Vic in was grotesque, but in a northern, woodsy way, not in a sun-baked desert way—she was pale and obese. Soft pouches of blubber fell from her chin, her upper arms and her waist, and in back, from her shoulder blades. When she gave Vic the key to room 11, his lucky number, he felt unlucky instead. Inside the room, there was an old console-model television with large round knobs. When Vic turned it on, the knob came off in his hand. He stared at the blank screen, feeling cut off, impotent, futureless.

"This here's your Class II rapids," Tom announced. "Everybody, stay in your seats. At all times, keep both feet on the

floor. Both hands on the safety rail. Everybody got that?" The passengers obeyed, Vic most anxiously of all, though he tried not to show it. He was fairly athletic—he could ski intermediate slopes and held his own on the company basketball team, but he'd never ridden the white water before. He held tight, then felt like a fool as the raft bumped gaily over a hundred feet of mildly churning river.

Then the water was smooth and glassy again. Vic leaned over the side of the raft and watched the riverbed roll by beneath them. He could see straight through to the bottom. He dangled his hand in the water, surprised that it was ice-cold. He let his hand trail in the river until his fingers grew numb. A body leaned up against his. "Come here often?" the talking woman said.

The second rapids were a Class IV. Vic was sitting on the front bench now, trying to avoid the talking woman. The ride up front was bumpier. With every slight dip in the river, cold water slapped Vic's arms, and once, a wave appeared, seemingly out of nowhere, and doused him to the waist. The front was the place to be. Vic felt refreshed when he was wet. The women he was sitting next to started to tell him about their corporation. They were correcting each other, competing.

Unattached working women in their thirties were the same everywhere, even at the bottom of the Grand Canyon—fatigued by years of dating, but still fiercely determined. Vic wore no wedding ring. He was fair game. He decided to mention his girlfriend to clarify his status. "My girlfriend's a movie publicist," he said. "She met Billy Crystal. He's very nice, a regular guy."

Horror registered on the women's faces. "Yeah, right," one said. "We need more of those." They all fell silent.

Vic felt he should leave. He moved back to the middle bench and sat next to the Germans. They introduced themselves. They were retired, they told Vic, and unmarried. They spent their time traveling. They described their six months in the Caribbean, sailing around the Virgin Islands. "The sunsets," the man said in his Arnold accent. "Unbelievable!"

"Forget about it," said the woman.

"One night, we saw a UFO," the man said.

"You saw it first." She patted him on the back.

The talking woman spotted Vic. She squeezed across from the Germans, talking about her medical bills. The medical students, who were sunning themselves in gorgeous French bathing suits, turned to listen. Even Tom was interested—he stopped fiddling with his thermometer. Everyone liked hearing about the disasters of the health care system in America.

Thousands in medical bills were owed, the talking woman was saying. Something was always happening to her. The bills for her last injury were coming in up to a year late and Blue Cross was declining. Where the money would come from, she had no idea.

"Heck," Tom said. "If Kathy gets a snakebite, I suck it out. If I get one, she sucks it out. That's the only medical insurance we need."

A blank, white heat enveloped the slow-moving raft. The brightness ate the color from the cliffs as they swept past. The water surface was all reflection. Vic closed his eyes. His brain was hot. It was happening—his personality was disintegrating. There were private, unlovable eccentricities which he kept hidden and which threatened to surface—a rigid solemnness, a secret delight in poor personal hygiene, a corny sense of humor, an obsession with homonyms. He wanted to be like Tom, the same thing inside and out. Tom didn't melt in the heat; he burned true.

Lunch stop, people," Tom announced.

Vic's legs were stiff. He was unsteady on his feet. So were the others. Everyone complained as they jumped awkwardly down from the rim of the raft onto the hot sand. There was a

narrow strip of beach edged with feathery, waist-high chartreuse grasses. “There’s a surprise in there,” Tom said to Vic.

Vic wandered like a zombie into the cove. The rocks there were a mellow amber, the color of fine Italian leather. Streaks of white travertine marble looked brushed on by hand. The scale of the cove was human, a comfort compared with the cosmic scale of the canyon. Vic was touched—the surprise was a waterfall. He took a turn under the falls. The water was cold, hard and forceful. For a moment, it pounded his personality back into him, then that Vic was gone again.

At the sandwich buffet, he assembled a monstrous turkey, sprouts, tomato, provolone creation with everything on it. He ate, standing alone.

The talking woman was wading. Her bikini was an old, tired one with a twisted lining. She was thick as an oak tree through the middle, her breasts like small burls.

Tom was watching her. He sat Indian style on the sand while Kathy massaged his neck and shoulders. Vic brought a Heineken over and squatted beside them, drinking it. “Nice surprise, this cove,” Vic said.

“You’ll never see a prettier one.” Tom’s face inflated slightly with pride.

“How’d you get into this?” Vic asked Tom.

Tom told his story. He’d herded sheep since he was yea-

high. He'd been raised by his grandparents. One of his folks had an alcohol problem. Part of ranch life he liked. He liked seeing lambs born. A shepherd had to be vigilant. If the ewe gave birth in the shade, her kid would freeze to death. Tom had to carry the newborns into the sun. The ewes didn't like that. They followed him, butting him in the shins. Celebrations on the ranch, he also liked. They'd make a huge fire, slaughter a goat. The waste came pouring out. They'd throw the head on the fire. Eat the intestines and everything. Food was sacred. Nothing was wasted. Not like the Anglos. But, soon as Tom was old enough, he got away. He'd always known, since he was small, there was only one place he wanted to be and that was the river.

When Vic was sure the story was over, he said, "I'm from Ann Arbor."

"We get people from all over on this trip," Tom said; he showed no further curiosity about Vic. The talking woman was now in water above the waist. "You," Tom called. "Come back. You're too far out."

"Me?" The talking woman pointed at her expansive breastbone with both index fingers.

"You," Tom called. She obeyed. The other passengers set aside their sandwiches to watch. The talking woman tried to swim straight to shore, but the current forced her slightly

downstream with every stroke. Kathy rose, ready to act, but Tom motioned for her to stay put. They watched the talking woman drag herself ashore.

"Drinks like a squaw, that one," Tom said. "She's had what, two six-packs already? We don't get that element on the eight-day. This one's for softies. The eight-day—you'd like that. That's more your style." He gave Vic a man-to-man nod.

"Is it?" Vic said. He wanted to be whoever Tom thought he was. He wanted to do well on the Colorado.

Okay, people, she's a hundred and fifteen," Tom said, checking the thermometer. They were back on the river, barely moving. The cliffs towering over them on either side shimmered with heat. "We got smooth water. It's a good time for you to lie down and sunbathe," Tom said. "If you get too hot, ask Kathy for the bucket. She'll pour water on you, cool you right down. Or try the turban trick. Dunk your towel in the river, wrap it around your head."

Vic spread his towel out on the wide canvas rim and lay down. He hoped the talking woman was tired after her swim and would sleep. No such luck. She was talking to the French girl about raising a retarded child. Her daughter was twenty-six years old and still living at home. "They can be very will-

ful," the woman said. "You don't know when to push them and when not to. Sometimes they understand more than they let on. If I don't watch mine, she gets her way about everything."

It was time for Vic to try the turban trick. He dangled the towel in the water. It grew heavy quickly—the river almost yanked the sodden terry cloth from his hand. He wrapped his head and lay back down. He closed his eyes. His mother was the opposite of the talking woman. His mother was beautiful, thoughtful, polished, intriguing, a natural focus of men's attention. It was she who had encouraged him to iron the eccentricities out of his personality, so he would be smooth, crisp and flawless as blue oxford cloth. She thought he'd do better that way. He probably had. He felt a pang. He really wanted to see the lake again. Maybe they would drive up to the Upper Peninsula together. Every summer of his childhood, the three of them had gone to the lake. It was cool and green and lazy there. A boy could spend all day in a boat.

Vic dreamed of two men from the UP who were friends of his father's. He hadn't thought about them for twenty years. They had more character in their little fingers than a whole corporate division had today. They would stand on the dock on summer evenings with his father talking wryly, knowledgeably, of the way things were built of wood. The ultimate was a thing with no nails. Even in his sleep, a sob formed in

Vic at the thought of a thing with no nails. Gus Reese. Onnie Tuner—what was Onnie short for? The faces of those men, their soft voices and what they knew seemed precious and lost forever. All of them were dead. His father had gone first, buried in a coffin built by Onnie and Gus, dovetailed cedar—the ultimate thing with no nails.

Something cold and metallic brushed against Vic's arm a few times, then rested there, stirring him gradually awake, causing his clear, mysterious dream to vanish. He opened an eye. The cold thing was a can, Coors Light. Vic reared up. The talking woman had commandeered the top two feet of his towel. Her mouth was moving. Thank God for the turban—he couldn't hear her. Was anyone listening? The French girl was asleep. Everyone else had his back turned. Everyone looked uncomfortable, stiff, hot, thirsty, lonely, mortal. Vic lay back down. Perhaps they were all disintegrating.

The raft moved sluggishly downstream. The light had lengthened and the cliffs looked like magnificent, baroque sand mansions, with dark arches of shade for windows. Vic fantasized crawling up and living in one. He was hallucinating. At home in his closet, his exec self and his Lite Rock self hung on hangers, inhabiting their respective costumes. His mother

resided on her typed name card in the Rolodex at International Cookie. Only his father, at rest in his dovetailed coffin, was real.

One of Vic's arms was numb. He rolled over and felt a stinging sensation on his forearm. The tip of the talking woman's cigarette was brushing his skin. "Hey!" he yelped. "You're burning me!" The passengers turned to see what was wrong with Vic. "She burned me," Vic explained. He drilled the woman with a look of contempt.

"Oh my God," she said. "It's such a filthy habit. I keep saying I'll quit, but I don't. Here, let me make it better." She grabbed his forearm, brushed the black smudge off, and tried to kiss the skin. He yanked his arm away.

"Okay for you," she said. "You won't let me make it better. I'll burn myself to make up for it." She relit the cigarette. "There," she said, grinding it out on her forearm.

The passengers watched with pity, shrinking away. Vic was furious. She and he now had matching burn marks. Angrily, he moved to the rear.

"Now he hates me," the talking woman said. "Wahhh," she bawled a mock bawl. She reached for an unopened can of beer. It was wet. It slipped from her grasp and rolled slowly along the floor of the raft to the rear. "Here, kitty, kitty, kitty," she said, chasing the can. Vic watched her grab it up, sit down

on the rim of the raft, cross her legs and, throwing her head back to drink, lose her balance and almost fall overboard. Instinctively, he rose out of his seat, lunging forward to catch her, but she caught herself.

Vic was afraid of what he might become without his rules and restraints, his goals and his strict self-management. He once had let himself go, sophomore year in college, after breaking up with a girl, Francine. He'd gone into debt, stopped bathing, come within a hair of being expelled before he woke up and smelled the coffee. He had once been loathsome and he could become loathsome again, a hideous, malodorous freeloader perhaps, sitting on a park bench airing his feet and eating garbage.

"Vic," Tom said, "go up front. This here's your Class VII rapids, your best shot." Vic was pleased. He hadn't thought Tom remembered his name. He moved up to the front bench.

"Okay, people," Tom announced. "This one's a goodie. Everybody remember: feet on the floor, hang on to the rails, stay in your seats." The current picked up, pulling the raft aggressively forward. The roar of the rapids could be heard around the bend. The gorge narrowed; the river was constricted by the towering walls; it tore through the pass in

torrents. "Everybody: both hands on the safety rail," Tom called. "Here we go." The raft careened like a car skidding on ice.

Vic sat tight, his knuckles fused to the rail. The raft charged the white water, fishtailing, plunging, sailing through the air, dropping hard into the pocket. The impact sent a wave slamming into Vic. The water was so cold it tore a shout from his throat. The raft skidded again. Vic's head was spinning.

The second pocket was just ahead. He wanted to try something crazy, a ski-jump move. He rose to his feet as the raft dropped, raising his arms for balance. For a moment, he was flying. The raft fell out from under him. He took the icy wall of water head-on. The raft caught him. He was on his feet and fine. "Yes!" he shouted, punching the air with his fist, shaking the cold water from his head. "Yes!"

Water filled his eyes and ears. He was exhilarated. He wanted to give Tom the thumbs-up sign, to clamber back over the benches and talk about the ride. He wiped his eyes with the back of his hand and shook his head hard to get the water out of his ear. The other passengers were in an uproar. The German was jumping up and down on the bench, shouting in German and pointing back at the rapids. His lady friend translated, "Man overboard—he saw it first."

Vic was stunned. His stomach turned as he saw it, the head

bobbing in the white water a hundred feet back. "It's her," Kathy reported to Tom.

"I know who it is," he snapped. He flashed her a long, public, blameful look. The talking woman was overboard.

Tom turned the rudder hard, navigating straight across the river. The raft slipped backwards and sideways in the strong current, as he pushed the motor to bear the load upstream. A bank of rocks jutted out from the south wall of the gorge. Tom steered the raft around the rocks. Kathy dropped anchor. The water was calmer there, swirling in a slow eddy.

Tom slipped over the side into waist-high water. Laboriously, he waded upstream. The passengers gasped as the talking woman's head went down. The med students consulted each other in French. Tom moved steadily upriver. The water grew shallower. He was in up to his shins when the passengers cried out. The talking woman was coming downstream sideways. They watched, spellbound, as she bounced slowly over a stretch of small rocks, bumped hard into two big ones. She disappeared again when she hit the first pocket.

Something dislodged her and she rose to the water surface again, her body naked, white and vibrant in the blue water. The current pulled her sideways into the fast lane of the pass. Elastically, the body slipped into the second pocket.

Watching this, Tom knew she was dead. From deep in his

belly, he wailed a wail that made the hair on Vic's back stand up and pulled a sympathetic sob from a place as deep within Vic. The women clasped hands and wept. Kathy stood rigid, her face white.

The talking woman bobbed toward Tom on her stomach. Tom crouched like an athlete, shifting his weight from right to left and back to keep his footing solid. She glided manageably into his shins. Tom turned the talking woman over onto her back. He pulled her tongue out of her throat, closed her mouth, closed her eyes. The women passengers could no longer look. They turned away, consoling each other.

Vic watched Tom ease the body downstream. When the water level reached his thigh, he loaded the body onto his shoulders. He was straining under the weight, moving more slowly than seemed possible into the deep water where the raft was anchored.

He barked an order at Kathy. She hoisted the talking woman aboard. Out of water, the body looked deader than in. Her skin was blue, though as yet unbruised. The facial features were tight and well defined. Vic sobbed again—the talking woman was attractive. The medical students examined her, poking, prodding, pressing, confirming her death in jarringly elegant, technical French.

Tom peeled off his shirt. He was shivering violently. Kathy

tried to dry his back with a towel. He shunned her—he ordered her to wrap the talking woman. She asked the passengers to donate their towels. Ceremoniously, all terry cloth was handed to the rear of the raft. Tenderly, deliberately, Kathy wrapped the body from head to foot in a noisy collage of toweling, imprinted with Peanuts characters, the Coke logo, the American Express card.

Tom gave Kathy the nod; she raised anchor. Tom was tired. He guided the raft too slowly out of the eddying pool. The current pushed the raft back into the rocks. A horrible grinding screech sounded as the steel prop scraped the granite. Vic would never forget the sound of that screech echoing over and over against the walls of the canyon, the pitch rising, the string of syllables fusing slowly into one.

As the raft rounded the last bend and entered Lake Mead, Vic felt he was being released from the great, magnetic, centripetal hold of the canyon, the hold of Tom. He didn't feel ready to leave. He didn't like the looks of Lake Mead—it was an ordinary body of water, large and bright in the late afternoon light. Two old men were putting around in a motorboat, fishing poles put away for the day. An air-conditioned bus was idling on the far shore, waiting to transport the rafters back to the motel.

Vic wanted to comfort Tom, to say something important. He stayed behind when the other passengers disembarked. He helped carry the coolers and gear ashore. He wanted to help with the body, but Tom didn't need help. Vic last saw Tom and Kathy hauling the raft out of the water, breaking it down and loading it onto Tom's flatbed.

In the morning, Vic was wearing a suit and tie, flying home to Ann Arbor. He read *Newsweek* and looked out the window. *Munchies Mountain*. He would feel exposed, standing up in front of his team tomorrow and pushing the new concept. He was afraid a fall was coming. If you believe it, they believe it—that was his motto, it was how he got where he was. And he didn't believe it.

Suddenly, he remembered the talking woman burning him with her cigarette. He unbuttoned the shirt cuff and slid his jacket up. There was the burn mark, a tiny eye in the flesh of his forearm. He touched it. It was still hot.

Close

Families with teenage suicidals were Jorie's specialty. She had ways of working with them. She functioned like a conduit, channeling information from parents to children and back, but she enhanced the information slightly in its passage, so that when it reached the offending generation it could be heard and seen in the best possible light. Her favorite device, after listening to both sides and arriving at a stalemate, was to conclude that this daughter so respected the stated and unstated laws of the parents that, unable to honor those standards in her life, she felt she had no alternative but to honor them with her death. It was in some ways a tribute. Quietly offered by Jorie, this interpretation sent some of the hardest

families crumbling, brought soft tears to the most rigid of patriarchs. Love—love that had been driven into hiding—came dancing out toward its object, eager and nimble, free at last. That was when it worked. Sometimes the love included Jorie; other times the family developed a post-crisis loathing for her. She was evidence of the painful past which they never wanted to see again. She felt like the bloody clothes of an accident victim left behind for the hospital to discard. What do I want from them, she asked herself, a pat on the head? A plaque?

She had accepted an invitation to speak to teenagers at the Suicide Conference in Vancouver. The incidence there was especially high among Indian and Pakistani teens, Romeo-and-Juliet couples. They were children of MTV, falling in love, experimenting with sex, yet they were expected to submit to arranged marriages. With this kind of couple, Jorie's device worked well. In the past, she had been too busy to accept other similar invitations, but this one had been issued for June, when her time would be her own. It was to be an easy, unfettered summer. Her sons from her first marriage and her stepdaughters would all be away on programs and trips, and she had asked for and been given leave from her part-time job as a social worker at New York Hospital. Until the conference had come up, she and her husband, Paul, had considered vis-

iting members of her family—nieces in Dallas, parents in Phoenix, a brother, Jan, in San Francisco. When the Vancouver dates were confirmed, they changed their plans. Paul would fly out from New York to join her at the conference, and they would then drive the Trans-Canada Highway to Lake Louise. It made sense.

Arriving in her hotel room at midnight, Jorie read and reread the notes from the case study she would be discussing. It concerned two sisters, twenty-seven and nineteen. The older was physically handicapped and had been the exclusive focus of the parents until a series of suicide gestures by the younger. Jorie was trying to plan pauses and inflections for the maximum in dramatic effect. Yes, she realized as she dozed off, I do want a plaque.

The telephone rang at ten after six—her wake-up call, she thought—but the angry voice belonged to Theo, her older brother, calling long-distance from Dallas. Jan had died in the night. He had contracted AIDS seven months earlier and had not let anyone in the family know. Jan's lover, Hank, was following instructions: tell Theo, get Theo to call Jorie, have Jorie call Mom and Dad. Jan wanted to be buried in Bloomington, Indiana, where the family had lived when he was a boy. Jorie's hand felt fused to the receiver as she hung up. She couldn't lift it again to do what Jan had wanted her to do. Her

reflection in the hotel mirror—lips stoic, eyes betrayed —remained her only memory of Vancouver.

Once her ticket to Indiana was in hand and her luggage was gliding away from her on the conveyor belt, she scanned the terminal for a pay phone. There were five booths in a row, all empty. She felt the need of something well made and long-lasting beneath her—a religious foundation, philosophical underpinnings. Instead of calling Phoenix, she called Paul. Her voice came out a whisper with a hint of pitch; she was holding back chaos. Paul did all the work. "Jorie. Theo told you?"

"Yes."

"Do you want to talk about it?"

"No."

"Did you call your folks?"

"No."

"Do you want me to?"

"Yes."

"Where are you?"

"In the airport."

"I'm on my way. See you in Bloomington."

• • •

From her seat by the window in the first row in coach, Jorie watched the stewardess serve a beautiful golden cocktail to a man just ahead of her in first class. It was 7:40 A.M. She wanted a cocktail too, but first she had to figure something out. What had happened and how had it happened? Had seven months gone by without her hearing Jan's voice? She had sent a Christmas card, left a birthday message on his answering machine in March. He would have told her. Even if he had planned not to, she would have heard something in his voice, she would have asked, he would have told her. Somehow, communication between all of them had become infrequent and superficial. Jorie remembered the fortieth-anniversary party. Her folks had just moved to Phoenix; she had recently separated from her first husband; Jan had just come out and brought his lover with him. Everyone had worked around the tension, but the effect was so toxic that in the six years that had elapsed since then, no further holiday reunions had been suggested.

Jorie picked up the in-flight magazine to distract herself. Thumbing through it back to front, she stopped to study the world map of airline routes. The map made it all look like a snap: bright-green continents, bright-blue oceans, laced with red arcs, planes skipping merrily over the surface like stones on a still lake. Jorie's stomach turned over. Everyone was too

far apart. Everyone was in a different state; the children were all in different countries. No one in any of her families—nuclear, extended, reconstituted—was home. She felt the need to hold everyone together. She placed her little finger just outside Zurich, where one son was visiting a Swiss farm family. Her thumb easily reached the blue waters of the Virgin Islands—her younger son was there on a sailboat with his father. She wished that she could connect herself to her two sons without including their father, but that was not possible. With a little cheating, her middle finger could stretch home to LaGuardia, to Paul. No fingers were left for his daughters, vacationing in Denmark with their mother, but that would be fine with them. Her right hand looked deformed, splayed over the right half of the map.

Now for the left page. She located herself, tracing the red line a quarter inch, from Vancouver to Calgary. The other family members could only be connected by resting her entire palm over the West. They would all be in Bloomington by late afternoon, waiting for Hank and Jan. Jan's request to be buried in Bloomington was filling the skies with family, following their red arcs home, even though no one lived there anymore. They would be collecting at the funeral parlor in their old neighborhood, driving to the cemetery on Windhill Road, passing their house. If the new people had done any-

thing to the porch, Jorie would be upset. The best of family life had happened on that porch. Why hadn't Jan let them all fly the other way, to San Francisco, to help take care of him? Theo had been furious. "I want to know who he got it from," he raged on the telephone that morning. "If he got it from Hank, I'm going to have a big problem. I'm going to want to kill him."

"Please," Jorie said. "Please don't ask Hank who got it from whom."

"Why the hell not?"

"Because," Jorie said, and she went on to repeat to her brother everything he had told her in outrage, but with a saintly twist. "You said Hank made sure he never lacked for visitors. Hank made sure he had painkillers. Hank helped him write a will. Hank did it all, right to the end."

"I would have done it too, only nobody asked me."

"But that's not Hank's fault."

A wave of queasiness rocked her stomach again. "Was that turbulence?" Jorie asked the young man in shirtsleeves next to her, but he couldn't hear. He was plugged into the twelve-channel audio system. "Was that turbulence?" she called to the stewardess, two rows behind her, serving coffee from her cart.

The man in first class whose 7 A.M. cocktail Jorie had

admired turned in his seat to answer her. “Nope.” He smiled. “No turbulence yet.” He watched her a moment, his smile dimming. “Are you okay?” She nodded, keeping her hands firmly on her family members, holding them together.

Jorie had met Hank once. Hank had scrutinized her triumphantly, as if he knew things. Had she done horrible big-sister things to Jan that she didn’t remember? Her male clients sometimes complained about their big sisters. Perhaps there was less intention in all this covert family brutality than she had encouraged them to believe. How could she make up for hers? Jorie did not know how to think of Jan now. Jan had been very intense, very elusive when he was alive; he would probably continue to be so now that he was dead. But where would he continue? Would she have more answers if she had been with him more? She had always described her family as close. Was it possible to feel close, very close, to someone who didn’t feel close to you? Yes, it happened all the time. She could think of three specific middle-aged clients who still longed for signs of affection from older siblings who couldn’t care less.

Jan was a vegetarian. Jorie remembered how he had given up pork at age ten, after seeing a certain pig at the county fair. The pig had looked him in the eye so intelligently, he had said,

that it was as if the pig were a man trapped inside a pig. The family accommodated him easily—a little less bacon in the skillet on Sunday morning. Chicken came later and was more inconvenient. Jan was watching Mom cut up a fryer. The sight of the blood running where she sliced apart the blue sockets of the leg bones made him lose his appetite. Mom adjusted by preparing bigger salads, a second vegetable, a plate of cheese. For Jan, she learned to cook fish, frozen slabs from the supermarket, unless a neighbor brought fresh fillets home from a trip north. Finally, when they were all grown and living in different cities, Jan gave up fish. Jorie had witnessed the moment. She was sitting next to him at the local fancy restaurant one weekend when everyone had returned to Bloomington for an important wedding. She was in her first marriage, careerless, dazed with her own insignificance. Theo had completed his Ph.D. thesis on Joyce and couldn't find a job; his wife was expecting. Jan had a mistrustful, embarrassed quality. He was a senior at Berkeley, majoring in art history. Jan had ordered the sole. The waiter brought everyone's entree with a great flourish. Jan's was last. Jorie remembered wondering if the waiter was gay. "Lucky boy," he said to Jan with pride, "your sole was very, very pregnant and we left in the roe. Enjoy."

There was a nice conversation going on, Jorie thought,

between her mother and her sister-in-law about babies. She glanced at Jan. He had pushed his main plate away untouched. He had removed and balled up the foil from his baked potato and was slicing it into neat strips and chewing methodically, the way most men would eat a steak. For some reason, Jorie did not want her mother and father to realize what was going on. It wasn't so much the high cost of the meal, given their means, as they might feel a sense of failure as parents—an inability to nourish and satisfy. Without asking Jan, she mussed his plate with her fork so it would look used. He stopped chewing to watch her. She tried to disguise her intent by ingesting the roe, the entire, sickeningly rich, slimy, chewy, dense crescent of eggs. Always between, she thought now. I'm always between people, trying to minimize harm.

The captain's voice came over the loudspeaker, announcing that they were flying over the Canadian Rockies. Jorie's shoulders stiffened, and she turned her back to the window. The last thing she needed right now was to look down on the tops of some of the highest mountain peaks in the world. A terrible panic seized her. It seemed like a bad idea, flying. How did these big boats stay up, anyway? The world was full of things

that she didn't understand but had to depend on—all bad ideas. People should be taught how things work. Electricity, telephones, televisions, cameras, submarines, rockets, everything. Life was too full of anxiety when you had to take everything around you on faith. Oh God, she thought, wherever you are, you have to take it on faith. Jan has to take his world on faith, wherever he is. Where is he? If he's not in his body, is he in the air? Is he like smoke—elusive, tender, vegetarian smoke? If so, she was probably closer to him now than before when he was in San Francisco and she was in New York. In fact, with the whole family thirty-five thousand feet in the air, they were all closer to Jan—as close as they would ever get. Emotion, sharp as cayenne pepper, filled the back of her throat, driving tears into her eyes.

A child behind Jorie began to sing a phrase from a popular song. The child had learned the phrase phonetically. It was senseless enough to begin with, but repeated over and over, it was almost unrecognizable as English. It sounded like a child of five or six, a boy. Turning to peer between the seats to see if she had guessed correctly, Jorie felt her lap fall out from under her once, twice, three times. The magazine slid to the floor. Her eyeballs ached. "Was that turbulence?" she called to the man in first class.

"Yup," he said. "That was it." He raised his index finger slightly, stopping the stewardess. Jorie watched as he quietly ordered two cocktails, one for himself, one for her.

There was more turbulence—a long series of violent belts of air against the belly of the plane. The seat-belt sign went on; the captain apologized. Jorie held her breath, but the plane did not lose altitude, did not plummet to the earth like a falling stone, breaking the red arc, blackening the green continent. Jorie was afraid, even when it was over. She did not want to die, to have thirty seconds of understanding, a few miserly illuminations, between herself and the end of consciousness. Two strong memories of the porch in Bloomington arose. In each memory it was dark and a brother was there: Theo coming home from college, reading aloud to her, "Do Not Go Gentle into That Good Night." Jan, as a beautiful eight-year-old, singing, "I'm an old cowhand from the Rio Grande."

Jorie was tired of fighting, tired of holding the door shut against pain. Pain was stronger, pain was hungrier. Pain would win this one. If Jorie didn't stand aside and let it in, it would break down the door. It was the marauder, there to loot her, to take whatever she had that it wanted. When it was gone, there might not be anything left. There was nothing she could say to stop it or change it. Her shoulders slumped softly into

the seat back, her hands fell open. *Come in*. To her surprise, the first rush was intimate and heady, with a precipitous edge, so close to pleasure that she thought, If I didn't know it was loss, I'd think it was love.

Part Two

The Drunk

Everyone in the subway car was standing with their backs to him, perhaps because he was talking to himself, calling Governor Cuomo a fascist nigger-lover. Although this is a crazy thing to say out loud in a subway car in which there are at least eight mature black guys wearing hidden handguns and one teen possibly packing a semiautomatic, I sat down in one of the many empty seats next to this man because I knew he wasn't crazy. Crazy I know.

There was a brief silence. He absorbed the fact that he hadn't intimidated me. "Nice boots," he said.

I hadn't anticipated this angle. "Thanks," I said. The boots were wine-colored cowboy boots with pointed toes and

clever black stitching, a stitching design that linked them historically to Arabia in the following reverse-chronological sequence: Texas-Mexico-Spain-Arabia. The introduction of horses to America follows the same sequence. Not many people know this, but horse cultures (cultures that evolve from economic systems that depend on horses for transportation, war, food-gathering or barter) produce folk dances with certain distinguishing characteristics. There is rhythmic stamping and clapping; footwork can be fancy. There is little use of the pelvis and the use of the arms is restricted to a plane roughly defined by the shoulders. Think Spain and flamenco. Think Texas and line dancing.

I thought of all this and could have told it to the man (except for the word *pelvis*, which could have been construed as a come-on) as we both gazed down with admiration at the toe of my boot, but I didn't want to send the conversation in that direction.

"Are they new?" he asked.

"They're two years old," I said. I thought that said a lot about the boots, the fact that they were two years old and an intelligent man on the subway thought they were new.

He *was* intelligent, which is why I sat down next to him despite his intentionally provocative mumbling. I can navigate safely among all types of people, never mistaking an eccentric

or a renegade for a truly crazy person. This man was a renegade, the kind who's too intelligent for his own good—he argues his way out of jobs and marriages, out of friendships, out of the soothing embrace of his own familiar neighborhood. He was in his fifties and Irish-American—he had the jaw, the chin, the pale blue, bitter, superior eyes. He was lanky and mean. He possessed the kind of calm that comes from a complete indifference. Life could take nothing away from him now but his pint, and that not for long. He had ways. He had means. I saw all this in a flash—in his posture, his clothing, his facial expression—as I entered the car, and subconsciously I determined he was not a threat and I could make myself comfortable sitting next to him.

"Do you hire a shoeshine guy to polish them?" he asked.

"No, I do it," I said. I was testing him, leaving myself open for a demeaning antiwoman crack. In my income bracket, I shouldn't be polishing my own shoes.

"No kidding!" He was excited. "Not many people polish their own boots. What do you use, saddle soap?"

"Yes."

"What kind of rag?"

"To tell the truth," I said. "Nothing works better than an old sock."

I was nervous about revealing the sock detail because,

mundane as the subject appeared to be, this detail was the height of intimacy to me. I had put together a strange little bag for shoe and boot care, the kind of bag where if this subway car crashed and I got killed and neighbors had to empty my townhouse, they would pick through the shoe-care bag with pity and mild horror—it was filled with old, formerly white, cotton socks stained the color of my shoe creams, black, navy, sandalwood, violet, cordovan. The cowboy boots got cordovan. Cordovan is the closest you can get to the color of wine.

The sock method was taught to me by my father who took excellent care of his shoes and who learned to do so in the Army, just like the man beside me. That's what he was telling me now, how he learned to polish shoes in the Army and how amazed he was that nowhere along the line had anyone mentioned using an old sock. Even a stretched-out old sock with a hole in the heel was the perfect soft, cotton mitten, the man was saying, for polishing shoes.

As he talked, I was reminded of other things my father learned in the Army: small-engine repair, celestial navigation, jungle survival skills. These things afforded him a lifetime of orientation. He tinkered happily in his spare time. He pointed out constellations. He could build a beautiful roaring fire anywhere, anytime, even in the rain.

What if, I thought to myself, we had protested the war but not the Army. What if we'd encouraged our men to go into the Army to change it for the better. They might have reversed it like they've reversed everything else. Look at how they do their own typing now. They change diapers. They arrange to alternate staying home with sick kids so their wives won't miss an important meeting or even just a day's pay. And they've lost none of their sex appeal. But they're cut off from something. And they suffer because of it. And because of that, God knows, so do we. It's not therapy we should be trying to talk them into, I concluded wildly, it's the Army. Be. All that you can be.

I was thinking about the Army as the man sitting next to me was describing how he used to polish his favorite pair of shoes, shoes he got in 1947, English-made saddle shoes which he called his black and tans. He had used an old diaper, working the tan areas first, proceeding from toe to heel, then working the black; he finished by buffing with a chamois. He threw in little tidbits linking the Truman administration to the fall of Chiang Kai-shek and the introduction of Koreans into the metropolitan New York economic equation as vegetable merchants. I was on the alert for anything snide in his voice, anything sinister or insinuating. The minute I heard anything I didn't like, the dialogue would end.

But he was sincere. At his most provocative, all he did was introduce slurs. He called the Koreans unscrupulous gooks, Chiang Kai-shek a slanty-eyed patsy, Truman a blockhead. What he was saying was smart. He tried to leave me in the dust by omitting pieces of his logic (the biggest being the consensual denial of the Korean War), but I followed him. It all related, every piece of what he said.

"Am I offending you?" he asked when he finished.

"Not yet," I said.

"Am I bothering you?" he asked. "Am I presuming too much?"

"Not yet," I said.

"You're nice," he said. "You know that of course. Everyone tells you you're nice and you know it without them telling you." I smiled at him a smile that said, Don't say another word and we'll always be friends. My favorite conversations with people end with a little silence. To help this silence along, I went into my resting-my-eyes act. I leaned my head back against the map of the New York City subway system and closed my eyes. The man cooperated. He folded his hands in his lap and sat quietly.

I hated it when a conversation got repetitive or personal or simply wouldn't end. I hated it most when people asked me where I lived. I live in a townhouse on the East River. I should

be taking cabs at this hour, but I don't take cabs because I might meet my son.

He drives a cab. He's driven a cab for eight years. Before that, he did telemarketing for two years. Before that he lived with me and watched television in his bathrobe for three years. When he lived with me I stopped going out, seeing people, doing things. And I didn't even know it. I thought I was busy.

Friends who've ridden with my son tell me he drives in fits and starts, he breathes in bursts, he watches you hard in the rearview mirror. Before you get out, he hands you a six-page memorandum, neatly word-processed, xeroxed and stapled. He has hundreds of copies piled next to him on the front seat. The title: "All That Is Necessary for the Triumph of Evil Is for Good Men to Do Nothing."

In the text, my son explains that since 1985, a group of Korean merchants has been trying to kill him. Many people project on the Koreans. To this end, these merchants have (a) taken his picture and distributed it; (b) circulated lies regarding his sexuality, lies based on "a deliberately selective interpretation of an inadvertent encounter." He explains. He met a woman in a bar who seemed to find him "irresistible." She asked him to accompany her home. There he received "two shocks." First, she tried to get money out of him. Second, she

revealed she was a he. Since then, my son estimates, "approximately 400,000–500,000 people acted out against him directly in some fashion." He acknowledges that the number seems high and explains his accounting method. He "counts people, not incidents," and gives this example: "If, in a group of five, one shouts *faggot*, but all laugh, he counts five."

Name-calling and threats are the most common forms of acting out, he says, along with spitting. He describes a variation on the spitting theme, "favored by many women and anal retentive men—a conspicuous clearing of the throat or a subdued but directed cough."

What he wants, what he asks for on page six, is names. If any of his passengers have heard about him and "are prepared to say so in a short telephone interview," it's proof of the conspiracy. Three years I listened to this. Three years I walked around on eggshells, afraid of the effect of everything I said to him, everything I did. Then suddenly, just like that, I wasn't afraid anymore. Of anything or anyone. One day he went out to buy cigarettes and while he was at the newsstand, I had the locks changed.

The subway rolled into the Seventy-seventh Street station. The doors opened. "Good night, my friend," I said to the man. He was genuinely sorry to see me go. Just before the doors jerked shut again, he saluted me, saying, like a perfect gentleman, "Thanks for talking to a drunk."

Release

Leaning forward, elbows on knees, Mike sat in a blue plastic bucket chair in the lounge. He had a rough, appealing face in the half-handsome, half-ugly vein. His sports jacket was too tight under the arms; there was sweat on his forehead. He exuded physicality. It was easy to imagine him ripping off the jacket to make love to a woman or to join in a brawl. But right now to Mike everything was upside-down and backwards. His fourteen-year-old daughter had ended up here in the adolescent wing of Boston Psychiatric. He'd come to visit her every day for the past two weeks. Now she was getting "out," moving to another city-run facility with one lock on the door instead of three.

The walls of the lounge were painted orange, a tentative

orange, as if to say, Cheer up, but not too much. The windows were barred. A donated baby grand occupied the corner. Next to it was an off-balance, yellowing palm plant. The room would have looked better with a glossy, green palm or, lacking that, no palm at all. The radio, a huge outmoded console model, was tuned to a disco station. A smooth, synthetic hit pulsed from the speaker, a Latin beat beneath high, idiotic words. A black girl danced by herself in front of the radio. Her body was chunky. Her hair looked burnt. It stuck straight out yet somehow failed at being straight. The dance she did was neither fluid nor sensuous; it was confrontational and arrogant.

A white boy with red hair padded about the lounge in bedroom slippers, slowly, heavily, as if he were blind or under water. The girl talking on the pay phone had skin the color and texture of coffee ice cream. Hot-pink yarn bows sprang out over shiny, black pigtails. She stood with her weight securely on one thin leg, cradling the receiver between shoulder and ear, winding her long slender arms around each other. "How's Johnny?" she asked. "What's Johnny doing? How's Rita?"

Mike's daughter should not be in a mental hospital, let alone the same mental hospital as these girls. These girls had been raped, one by an uncle, the other by a stepfather. Both had slit their wrists. How could anyone get well here? Mike felt crazy himself just sitting in a bucket chair in the lounge.

Dell, Mike's ex, sat next to him. Dell wore soft, flowing skirts and finely crafted silver jewelry. On her face was a gentle, understanding expression. As she sat, Dell flicked a hand through the underside of her long hair. They'd been divorced six years. Mike did well—he built office buildings. He still supported Dell. She reached into his jacket pocket to remove a cigarette. He lit it for her. Dell took a few shallow puffs.

"Go see what's keeping her, will you," Mike said. Dell handed Mike her cigarette and he took over the smoking of it.

"Let me talk to Grandma," the girl on the phone said. "No, I don't want to talk to him. I already talked to him. I talked to him yesterday."

Upside-down and backwards. Mike made $180,000 a year, his ex had a house in Cambridge. He had a house in the suburbs with a yard, a dog, a full-time housekeeper. And his daughter was being released from a mental hospital and sent to live in a halfway house run by the city. Upside-down and backwards. That's how things went when the city started sticking its nose into certain people's business. Rusty wasn't crazy. She wasn't a Suicide Attempt. She was wild. Dell couldn't make her go to school. How could you *make* someone go to school?

The social worker entered the lounge, a clipboard beneath her bosom. Some women had tits, but in Mike's view, this

woman had a bosom—a big, uninteresting shelf. She was an energetic, nearsighted woman with a frank smile. She strode toward Mike. He rose, tucking his shirt in with both hands, wincing to keep cigarette smoke out of his eye. "We're reversing things," she said. "Your daughter is signing out first. *Then* Doctor Anders will see us. There was a problem with admitting. An emergency. We needed Rusty's room." Her voice was gay. Mike stepped away. The social worker moved closer. She seemed to like being physically close to him. "Be patient?" she asked, cocking her head severely to the right. Mike's eyes shut hard with frustration. "You look worried," she said. "Don't be worried. Rusty read the resident contract. She said the rules were not a problem."

Mike didn't get it. When he was fourteen and he ran away from home, his friend's family took him in. But when Rusty ran away, she ran to bad friends. She stopped going to school. The school sicced Social Services on Dell. Social Services told Dell that Rusty was a minor—if Dell couldn't keep her in school, Rusty would be sent to live with her father. When Social Services said that, Rusty threw an ashtray at the wall and ran out into the hall. She can't live with me, Mike explained, repeating what Rusty had been saying to him since the divorce. We're always fighting. She can't stand me. Social Services warned Dell to take charge—Rusty could be re-

moved from the home. Rusty could be confined. Rusty could be mandated to live in a halfway house. It was all legal.

The lounge door opened and Rusty came in. Her black leather jacket was fetishistically torn and painted. Mike's features softened foolishly, helplessly at the sight of his child. He sidestepped the social worker. He didn't want Rusty to see him talking to her.

Rusty slumped in a seat, adjusting the earphones of her Walkman, fingering the buttons of the slender metal case. Her hair was dyed blue-black; she wore it spiky on top, long and purposefully tangled in back. Her eyes were tough like Mike's; the set of her chin was Irish, inviting argument. Her Levi's were shredded at the knees. Under the threads, her thighs were the color of skim milk.

Mike positioned himself on the edge of the chair next to her and leaned protectively forward. "Where's your stuff?"

Rusty was staring into space. "This is not the tape," she said. She concentrated on the music; she looked unhappy. She ejected the tape, flipped it, inserted it again. She listened.

"Didn't you have stuff?" Mike asked.

She frowned, listening to the tape.

"Hey, I'm talking to you," he said.

"What." Her eyes remained unfocused.

"Stuff!" Mike raised empty hands. "Don't you have stuff?"

She blinked at him rapidly and distastefully, shrinking from his volume. "Yes, I have *stuff*. Do you have *stuff*?" Her voice was mocking. Something on the tape caught her attention. She punched the fast-forward button and listened for a moment. "Shit," she said. "I thought that was it. But that's not it. This is not it."

Mike reached toward the ashtray to stub out his cigarette. Rusty intercepted it with an air of challenge. The smoke behaved theatrically for her as she inhaled—distinct, blue curls lay in her open mouth. She swallowed them. She repeated the performance, then stubbed out the butt.

He removed another cigarette, tapped it against his thumbnail for a very long time, then tucked it over his ear. "Where's Mom?" he asked.

"Looking for my tape," she said. "It was the best, but *really* the best tape. My friends made it for me." At the mention of her friends, Mike's entire upper body tensed, as if he might have to punch somebody. He had to stand up to ward off the urge to hurt those people. Rusty took note, expressing disapproval by slumping deeper in the chair and turning the volume up.

"Fuckin' junkies," Mike said when his anger had run its course.

"What?" Rusty pulled the earphones out.

"Nothing," he said. "I'm not talking to you."

They *were* junkies. Not all. But some. The others were freeloaders and thieves. They lived in a house on Linden Street off Comm Ave. That was the house where Rusty went when she wouldn't go to school. It was the house Dell called when Rusty ran away from home after their fights. Three times in the last year, Dell had sent Mike to that house to bring Rusty home. It got physical, with Rusty kicking him, pounding his chest, screaming at him that she wanted to live her own life. He didn't care how much she hurt him or hated him. He wanted her out of that house. Bad things happened in that house.

Dell walked in with a soft, bulging, cotton bundle. "This is all I can find of her stuff," Dell said, offering it to Mike.

"Is my tape in there, Mom?" Rusty asked.

"No, sweetheart."

A sock fell out of the bundle. Mike picked up the sock. He was exasperated. He hesitated to take the rest of the bundle. "I brought her stuff over here in a duffel."

Dell turned to Rusty. "Where is the nylon shoulder bag Daddy got you?"

"How many suitcases have I bought her," Mike said. "How many duffels."

"It was blue," Dell coached her daughter.

Rusty groped through the contents of the bundle as Dell held it. A nightgown spilled onto her knee; a hairbrush fell out. Mike picked up the brush. He took the bundle, wadding it up in one hand as if to discard it.

"I can't believe I lost that tape," Rusty said. "Did you look in the bed, in the sheets?"

"Everywhere," Dell said. "I gave the new patient Daddy's phone number. I told her to call us if she finds it and we'll come get it."

"No!" Mike shouted.

Everyone in the lounge looked at him. "*Sheesh!*" Dell said.

"What's here after today stays here," Mike said. "I'm not coming back here. I hate this fuckin' place." Rusty looked pleased with her father. He had no idea why. When he tried to please her, he failed.

A horrible, nerve-racking sound erupted from the radio speakers. The red-haired boy was toying with the tuner, moving it past intelligible frequencies, lingering on blasts of static. He left the dial on static and sat down on the piano bench. The dancing girl swayed from side to side with her fingers in her ears. An aide entered the lounge and turned the radio off.

"Way to go, David," Rusty said to the redhead. David wouldn't look at her.

"Let me go look in the sheets again," Dell said. She left the lounge.

"David was my partner in ballroom dancing," Rusty said to Mike. "Can you believe your daughter learned ballroom dancing in a mental hospital?" He perked up—she was talking in a normal voice, no attitude. The smallest hint of progress in her replenished great hope in him.

"No—yes—that's great!" he said—too eagerly. She pulled back. He took the cigarette from behind his ear and lit it. Rusty tried to intercept it. This time he blocked her. "Buy your own," he said.

"Tell Johnny 'bye," said the girl on the phone. "Tell Rita 'bye. Tell everyone Carmel says 'bye." She unwound her lithe arms and hung up. David padded dreamily over to the phone, put in a quarter and dialed.

The social worker appeared in the lounge doorway, her bosom lying on the clipboard as if it were a dinner tray. Her head was cocked to the left now, as if it had clicked off the delay. "Doctor Anders is ready for us," she said.

Dell was already seated in a folding chair in the small windowless room. Mike and Rusty sat on either side of her. Mike was amazed: a psychiatrist at this level had to work in an unventilated room no bigger than an industrial storage closet. He had sat in this room on the edge of his seat for three hours the day he committed Rusty. He could hardly breathe. Whoever built this place didn't know what he was doing.

Dr. Anders was a young, blond hint of a woman in a white

coat. Her style was cool and brainy; her voice was sterile and hypnotic. She almost seemed to be asleep as she stated the purpose of the meeting. Dell reached for Rusty's hand.

"Rusty and I have talked," Dr. Anders said, seeming to address Dell exclusively. "And she knows I think she's bright, I think she's very loving, I think she's very loyal. She's also impulsive. And maybe a little stubborn." Mike felt confused— Rusty *loving*? Rusty was a rebel, pure and simple. She was selfish. She was driving her mother nuts with worry. What was loving about that? "She's told me she's prepared to accept the halfway house rules," Dr. Anders said. "So let's all express our concerns. Anyone?"

"I think Rusty needs a vacation from the job of making her parents be parents," the social worker said. Her voice was merry; her understanding gave her a sense of order and therefore pleasure. Mike wanted to blacken her eyes. "I think the parental system, Dell the Pushover/Mike the Rescuer, presents too real of a temptation to Rusty to cry wolf, to activate the system. A halfway house eliminates the temptation. Especially since if she runs away from there, our girl will end up right back here." She pointed at Dr. Anders's linoleum.

"Hello, Miss," Mike said to the social worker. "*She*." He pointed at Dr. Anders's brain. "Said *she*." He pointed at Rusty's brain. "Is not crazy. She said it in this room. Three days ago.

After the testing. That's why she has to leave here, because she's not crazy. So she's not ending up *right back here*."

"If she runs, the police will be involved," the social worker said defensively. "Once they pick her up, they bring her here. For reevaluation. And possible reassignment." "She's not coming back here," Mike said, low and vicious. "None of us are coming back here."

"What are your fears, Mike?" Dr. Anders asked.

"She's going to meet the wrong kind of people," Mike said. "I don't want her living in a place run by the city. She's got money. She's got two loving parents." A soft blush collected in Dell's cheeks as if she'd been singled out for praise. Dell had been an illegitimate child. She'd been given away at birth and raised by nuns. "This is not why I went into business for myself, this is not why I worked nights and weekends, so she could live in a place run by the city."

"Understandable," Dr. Anders said, stifling a yawn. "Dell?"

"I'm not worried about the kids she'll meet," Dell said. "They're good kids. They just haven't had *opportunities*. To grow up without *opportunities* doesn't mean you're bad." Rusty put her arm around her mother's shoulders, thinking of her mother's lonely childhood.

"Are there any concerns?" Dr. Anders asked.

Dell stroked a spike of Rusty's hair. "My daughter likes her

freedom," Dell said. "I don't think curfews will sit too well with my daughter."

Dr. Anders smiled. It was an event, a stone, smiling.

"Your mother loves you very much," Dr. Anders said to Rusty. Dell's already soft edges grew softer until she seemed as boneless and cuddly as a stuffed animal.

"You know your mother really loves you, don't you?" Dr. Anders said.

Mike didn't get it. Of course Dell loved Rusty. Love was Dell's thing. These people had no idea. They should have seen Dell when Mike fell in love with her. She was more beautiful, more enchanting than any creature he had ever seen. Mike thought Rusty would get sarcastic or tell Dr. Anders to go fuck herself. "Yes," Rusty said. "I know that. I know she really loves me."

"And your father loves you too," the doctor said. "Though his is the sacrificial kind of love." The word *sacrificial* snagged Rusty's attention. She looked at the doctor suspiciously, then slid her eyes sidelong up at Mike without moving her head so Dell could not see the focus of her gaze.

"What are *your* concerns about me?" Rusty asked Dr. Anders. Mike was surprised. Rusty was using Dr. Anders's vocabulary.

"My concern is this: you can't live with Mom; you can't live

with Dad; you don't quite belong with your scary friends; you don't quite belong with the adolescents who tend to do well in a halfway house. To be wrong everywhere is a lonely life. But I think right now you're as scared for you as your parents are. And I think no matter what it costs you personally, you'll force yourself to survive the halfway house to prove they love you."

"I can *prove* anything if I feel like it," Rusty said. Mike could see she felt tricked into saying this. He choked up. He was sitting on the edge of the folding chair, his brain razor-sharp as he watched his daughter struggle to twist free from the trap. So much responsibility was on her shoulders. Rusty fitfully picked at a thumbnail. The silence went on, taking the form of a consensus.

"To recap," the social worker said, shattering the silence. "The curfew is eleven on weeknights. Midnight on weekends. You sign out to go to school, sign in when you return. Your school advisor signs your pass. You share light housekeeping responsibilities. You share a room. Some of the young people are more troubled, some, like you, are less."

"But what if I don't *feel like* proving anything?" Rusty said, ripping the hangnails away from her thumbs.

Dell leaned over and fished around for her bag, a large leather shoulder bag stashed on the floor beneath her volumi-

nous skirts. She found it and lifted it onto her lap, tugging on the long, loud zipper. The sound physically hurt Mike, it was so distracting.

"You read the resident contract," the social worker said. "You said the rules were not a problem."

"I'm not saying the rules *are* a problem," Rusty said. "I'm saying, what if I don't *feel like* proving anything?"

"Any ideas—anyone?" Dr. Anders asked, making her voice sound dull and routine.

Dell rifled through her bag, banging together aspirin bottles, ink pens, little plastic jars of hand cream. She held the mouth of the bag open wide and stared hard into its depths. Mike found himself staring into it with her, as if to help her find whatever she thought she needed.

"I don't think we heard you," Dr. Anders said to Rusty. "Would you repeat that?"

"I could try living with my father," Rusty said.

Her words lifted Mike out of his seat. Suddenly, he was walking around the shrink's office, saying, "What just happened? What just happened?"

"Sweetheart," Dell said. "You can't live with Daddy. You always fight. You and Daddy can't stand each other." It was delivered like an order.

"I said *try*," Rusty said.

Dell swallowed twice. Grief filled her eyes. She lifted a spear of blue-black hair out of her daughter's face slowly, stalling. "If you go to Daddy's," she said, striving for a brighter tone, "you can come to me on weekends."

Dr. Anders looked at Mike. Here's a window for you, Mike, her eyes clearly said to him. I'm not telling you what to do—it's up to you. You can jump out and fly or jump out and smash yourself to bits on the sidewalk.

"No weekends," he said. He stood over Dell. Using the full reach of both arms, he made the baseball umpire's safe sign. "None. She goes to school, she comes home. Same rules as the city place."

Dell looked at Rusty as if expecting a tantrum, but Rusty was silent and still. Her eyes were on the floor as she rubbed the sore spots around her thumbs where she'd ripped away the cuticles.

"Sweetheart," Dell said to Rusty, her voice thick in her throat. "You really want to go to Daddy's?"

Rusty nodded without raising her eyes. She looked exhausted.

"Then you go. You go then," Dell said. She looked up at Mike as if his face were a new face, one she wanted to fix and remember in a crowd. "Do you have a tissue?" she said to him as if he owed her that much. "I can't find a tissue."

Suddenly, everyone was standing, everyone was leaving. Mike was rooted to the spot. His heart was breaking and he wanted to laugh. In a daze, he followed the clutch of women out of the office and down the hall. The social worker dropped back to talk to Mike. "I like what you said in there," she said. "It was hard to say but you said it." Mike had no idea what she was talking about. He tried to outwalk her, but she kept up. "It's going to be hard at first. Rusty will test you. But I think she's ready for this to work. I think everyone is ready for this to work."

Dr. Anders was unlocking the wide, windowless steel door that sealed off the Adolescent Wing. It took awhile. There were three complex locks. Mike hated that door. He couldn't wait to get past it.

"Dell," Mike said. "Get her stuff." He followed her back into the lounge. The black girl, the dancer, was now on the phone. Her skin was butter-smooth, her brown eyes soft and maternal. The girl with hot-pink bows in her hair was seated at the piano playing all the black notes in a row from bass to treble. David was leaning over the sounding board, watching the effect of the action on the piano strings. The small bundle was still there, a clump of personal effects balled up in a cotton nightie in a blue chair.

"There it is," Dell said, pointing. Mike picked it up with

reverence and bore it out of the lounge. Dr. Anders locked the steel door after him.

Mike wasn't sure how it happened; he wasn't sure when. At some point between the moment the elevator car landed in the hospital lobby and the moment he lit Dell's cigarette at the curb, Rusty ran. Mike turned around and she was gone. He watched her tear down the sidewalk, the spikes of her blue-black hair scratching the air.

Belief

For weeks I'd planned to walk humbly down to the dock on Lake Okoboji after chapel on this, the first night of Methodist Camp, to pray. I'd planned to pray at the end of the dock earnestly and from a deep despair—I'd read in *Power for Living* that this was the only emotional state that produced results. However, they'd announced in chapel we were to stay off the dock. Some of the boards were old and rotten. A boy had fallen through the summer before and sued. All Methodist campers had to take buses over to Lutheran Camp across the bay to swim. They hadn't fixed our dock. The fund established for buildings and grounds upkeep had been raided by unanimous agreement in order to aid children orphaned by the

earthquake in Mexico. I'd seen the earthquake on TV. A twelve-year-old Mexican girl drowned in the mud in front of millions of viewers. She was literally up to her neck in mud for hours while men tried to pull her out. In the end the girl died, right on TV, because her grandmother, who was dead and buried in the mud beneath her, had a death grip on her heel. While the girl was still alive, she chatted nervously with reporters. Her main concern was the math test she was supposed to take the next day. She was afraid she would fail it.

I walked up and down the shore now, very upset about the absence of the dock. The absence of a dock was shaking my faith. There was always going to be an emergency somewhere in the world. Were we going to fund relief operations every time a country's children experienced an earthquake, famine or flood, and never create a safe place for our own children to swim and pray?

It was a cloudy, humid night. Flies were biting my ankles and sweat was trickling down the back of my neck. Lake Okoboji, the first lake I'd ever seen, was Iowa's biggest lake. I wondered if all lakes smelled metallic and fishy and morbid. The water slapped tediously at the posts of the dock. It didn't sound like water—more like blue jeans with grommets tumbling in a clothes dryer. At Lutheran Camp across the bay, someone was playing old fifties rock and roll. The water car-

ried the sound perfectly. I could hear every scratch of the needle, every note of the rolling piano bass, every word of Fats Domino's sad tenor voice on "Blueberry Hill." Those racy Lutherans—they could dance. I might become one, I threatened God, if Methodist Camp didn't work out. I was here because I needed help.

I needed a place to cut myself. I was too tall for a girl and too flat. I liked to cut myself in my spare time, little slashes with the cleanest, sharpest blade on my Swiss Army knife, little interruptions I could control and still prove that I was here. Between the girls' bunks and the boys' bunks, there was a grove of tall pine trees. I started up the footpath that led into the grove, but stopped halfway. Some campers were already in there. I could hear them breathing hard and grunting and slapping wet clay or something that sounded a lot like clay. I sat on a boulder and rolled up the sleeves of my shirt. I got out my Swiss Army knife and gently slashed the skin up and down the inside of my left forearm. It was too dark to see the blood, but I could feel it oozing. I ran my fingers through it. It was me, 98.6.

Morning Bible History class was taught by Pastor Morris of Earlham, a meek man with a low forehead, a singsong voice and a finicky manner. He spoke on confidence. I had just read an article on confidence in *Power for Living*, which used events

in the life of Moses as an example. Pastor Morris also used Moses, citing the same events, how Moses grew up a prince in Pharaoh's house, but erred by killing a cruel Egyptian taskmaster in order to free the enslaved Israelites. The result was he ended up a shepherd in the desert for forty years, convinced he was a nobody. Only through the development of confidence did Moses get to the point where he could part the Red Sea and lead two million slaves out of Egypt.

After Bible History, I went to the administration building and placed a person-to-person collect call to Mother. I wanted to go home. Mother's phone had been disconnected. Already? She didn't have to do that. She could have talked to me—I would have let her talk me into staying. I just wanted to tell her a few things. I needed to talk, that's all. We were moving to a new state, Mother and me, starting a new life as soon as camp was over. Dad was staying behind to go to jail. I wasn't supposed to know any of this. Fourteen years old and they tell me nothing. Fortunately, my bedroom shared a wall with Mom and Dad's bedroom, and every secret thing they said to each other at night sprang through the plaster to me.

I walked straight to the grove. It smelled like a hamper in there. Littering the ground were a number of small, milky latex baggies, a pair of sweat socks, a bra, and a tortoiseshell barrette. I sat down on a cushion of pine needles and prayed.

I told God all the things I hadn't been able to tell Mother. I said my cot was hard and it sunk in the middle. I said the food was terrible, the margarine smelled like vaseline and the orange juice wasn't orange juice, it was Kool-Aid. The girls in my bunk were mean, I said, and I was getting off on the wrong foot with them. I paused. I thought about the map of Iowa our counselors drew on a big piece of white cardboard, showing the towns each girl represented. Des Moines, Maureen Jenx—that wasn't me anymore. Where am I from now? I asked God. If you really know everything, tell me or I'll cut myself. God was mum. I unzipped my jeans and got out my knife. I slashed my thighs deep and good.

There was an air of festivity in the bunk after lunch. Several girls had seen the pastor who was to teach afternoon Belief class. He was young, they said, and cute. Everyone was dressing up for him. They were working on their makeup. Hair was paramount. They brushed, they teased, they blow-dried. A girl named Sherry, a brunette from Charles City, wore a lovely gold cross on a chain. It looked so chaste with her scoop-neck blouse, nestled atop the crack between her big breasts. Everyone wanted to borrow it. I was revolted by their hypocrisy. I went to Belief class early to pray quietly in the first row.

Cute was not the word for John. John had moral magni-

tude. I'd read about it in *Power for Living* but had never seen it until now. Perhaps it went along with being Greek. He wore the black pants and white shirts required of pastors, but his pants were pegged, his shirts were short-sleeved and open at the neck to the second button. His eyes were dark and intense, with lazy lids, as if he were in a constant state of being both teased and relaxed by serious issues of faith. Instead of standing at the lectern like an authority figure, reading from a tedious mimeographed sheet, John addressed us in an entirely personal manner. He pulled up a wooden stool and sat before us empty-handed. He spoke angrily, he spoke passionately, he spoke from the heart.

"Unwavering belief is for the strong, not the weak." John said it as if we'd disappointed him by showing up. "God never stops testing you; he just changes the level. After twelve years in the ministry, I am no more secure in *my* belief," he said, pressing his hands firmly against his chest as I too longed to do, "than you are in yours." His eyes looked tortured; spit flew from his lips. "Examine your hearts," he said, "for the flame that will burn true, that will tell you what is right and what is wrong. Otherwise, there is always the danger that you will let other people decide these things for you. If I have anything to say about it, you won't."

We were stunned.

"John, John, John!" Girls wept in groups for his love that night. They planned the next day's outfits; they experimented with their grooming. I was sickened. He said examine your hearts, not your hair. One girl with a twelve-color ballpoint pen copied the Bible verse John had cited from Ephesians in her notebook in each color, even yellow, which was invisible, then cradled the notebook in her arms and kissed her writing.

Sherry, the brunette with the gold cross and chain, was the only one mature enough to think of John as just another adult. "John has a four-door Mercury sedan," she said, matter-of-factly. "Caribbean Green. He's from Adair."

"How do you know?" asked one of the girls.

"I asked," Sherry said. She was trimming her hair in front of a 3" × 5" purse mirror, using only a pair of manicure scissors. "Why are you trimming your hair again tonight?" I asked.

"My magazine said to," she said, "to produce a wispiness about the face. Without the wispiness, I look chubby. See, the top half of my face is fuller than the bottom." She stopped trimming and held her face still so we could observe the imbalance.

"Where is that magazine?" I asked. I wanted to see if they had anything in there that would help me. Sherry handed me her *Seventeen*.

I read her *Seventeen* from cover to cover by flashlight on my

cot. The only thing in there I needed was a Marc Eden Deluxe Model Breast Developer. I wanted to believe it would work but I could see that the three Befores were not any different than the three Afters. What made the Befores look smaller was the slumped shoulders and protruding stomachs. The Afters threw their shoulders back and sucked in their stomachs. In terms of actual bursting, pendulous tittiness, inch for inch, the Befores and Afters were the same. They were liars and frauds. It should have been an ad for posture.

The sky over Okoboji was humid and close. The water was not visible from my window, but I could smell it, cold as steel, mossy and deep. It smelled like death. I inhaled deeply—I'd read in *Power for Living* that thoughts of your own death can spark profound spiritual revelations. This smell sent me up to the grove to cut myself.

The next afternoon in Belief class, John challenged us. "What," he asked, pacing before us with his dark eyes flashing, "is the difference between charity and pity?"

I raised my hand. I said sometimes acts of pity could be selfish.

"Ahh, Maureen. That's interesting." John was pleased. "Explain to us what you mean."

I told about Teresa, a Latvian girl I pitied because she had only one skirt and one blouse and she wore them to school

every day. Kids teased her. When they asked her why she always wore the same skirt and blouse, she said it was because the other ones she had—and she had dozens—were too good to wear to school. I felt so sorry for her that I brought a bag of my old clothes to school to give to her. She was hurt. She realized that all along the kids had been teasing her. She refused the clothes and she didn't come to school for a week. However good my intentions, I had done something selfish, I said.

John smiled at me, telegraphing a special man-woman love that warmed me to the depths of my soul. He addressed the others. "Does everyone understand the distinction Maureen draws?" He walked over to me and took a handful of my blouse, the yoke part over the shoulder. I almost died. "What if Maureen had taken off this green blouse?" he said. It was blue. Men can't tell the difference between green and blue. "And given it to Teresa? And said, 'May I wear yours?' The gift would not make Teresa feel inferior. If you give as a superior, it's an act of pity. If you give of yourself as an equal, it's an act of charity. Charity includes love and respect. Give with love, it will be received with love."

He patted my shoulder—I smelled cigarettes on his fingers. His black pants were at eye level. As he walked away, I wanted to grab hold of one of his legs, to force him to drag me

with him wheresoever he should go from that moment on, as long as we both shall live.

"John, John, John!" I sobbed into my cot after class.

That night, the girls sat around the lodge watching Sherry trim her shag and instead of talking about what outfit to wear to Belief class next, they tried to think up questions for John that would bring as much praise and shoulder-patting to them as he'd heaped on me. I stood half-in, half-out of the room, leaning against the doorway, listening.

"How about this?" said the girl with the twelve-color pen. She read from her notebook, "John, if someone killed my mother, can I hate them or would I be breaking a commandment?"

"Don't say kill your mother," someone said. "You might make it happen."

The girl crossed out *mother*. "Who should be killed—teacher?"

"John is your teacher!" Sherry said. "Don't kill him. He's got a wife and two kids. A boy, Todd, seven, and a girl, Nicole, four. Todd has a disease. I forget what."

When did Sherry ask John these questions? Not in class. Probably afterwards. She always stayed behind when the rest of us went back to the bunk.

"He's got a mother that lives with him, too," Sherry said.

"She came over from Greece. She misses it." She was holding a lock of hair taut and pulling the scissor blade against the grain to shag it. "John receives an average of four to six letters a week," she said. "Some are from girls in this bunk."

The girls looked right at me. So I wrote him letters. What was wrong with inviting him to my home for dinner, should he ever find himself in Des Moines. They were proper letters, very proper. One I signed *Love*. What was wrong with that? He told us to give with love.

"How old do you think John is?" Sherry asked. The guesses ranged from twenty-two to forty.

"He's thirty," she said.

"How do you know?" someone asked.

"I saw his driver's license." She put on her makeup carefully. She sprayed her neck with cologne.

"Where are you going?" two girls asked in unison.

"To my room. To read."

Alone on my cot that night, I said my prayers, skipping God and praying directly to John. I lay there afterward, smelling the lake, still as cold and steely as death. I sat up to get dressed and sneak up to the grove. Out my window, I could see a tiny orange dot glowing in the dark, moving toward our bunk from the direction of the grove. It was a cigarette, smoked no-hands, by someone who hugged her windbreaker around her

with both arms as she walked. Her face was tilted saucily up to the night. It was Sherry. That was the kind of woman I wanted to be when I grew up, one who smoked no-hands and walked around in the dead of night with her face high and saucy, one who didn't stay inside just to keep people from saying, where does she think she's going at this hour? Sherry climbed up on an orange crate and slipped into her room through the window. Her perfection took the wind out of my sails. I decided to wait until morning when it was good and light to cut myself—I'd skip Bible History.

I did a real job. I did my ankles. They bled so much the blood soaked all the way through my white socks. I ran back to the bunk to change my socks before the blood started to congeal around those white cotton fibers. All the girls in the bunk except Sherry were in my room, reading something and laughing. "What's that?" I asked. No one said anything. "May I see what's so funny?" I asked. Silence.

They left. I looked for my recent letter to John. I'd written him, pledging for the rest of my life to undertake private devotions for an hour each morn. I think I said morn. I think I said other, more personal things. The letter was long. I looked all over for it, under the pillow, between the sheets, behind the bed. I missed lunch looking for the letter. I unpacked my suitcase, shaking out each item of clothing. I went

through the wastebasket. I remade the bed. That letter was meant for John and John only.

In the excitement, I had forgotten to change my socks. When I remembered, it was too late—scabs had formed. I ripped the socks off, opening the wounds again, deeper now than when I'd cut them. Blood oozed out all over the floor. I mopped it up with a towel. I felt faint. I wondered if I should go over to the infirmary to see the nurse. If I did, I would miss Belief. I could not miss Belief. I pulled on a pair of black socks so John wouldn't notice my ankles were bleeding. I walked to chapel slowly, stopping to lean on a tree whenever I felt faint.

"Let's compare old beliefs with new beliefs," John said, seating himself on the stool with a big yawn. He was going easy on us this afternoon. "Everyone take a turn. Stand up and state something you no longer believe. Explain what new belief you've replaced it with."

The girl with the twelve-color pen mentioned Santa Claus. "That's one example," John said.

Another girl mentioned the facts of life. She told us she used to believe that newborn babies were found under the leaves of the cabbage plant. Now she knows that babies are the product of a man's sperm joined with a woman's egg. I don't know why she had to bring that up. It was the first I'd heard of

it. I had skipped Hygiene—I hid out in the girls' bathroom to cut myself.

I raised my hand. I told John that I used to believe people would do whatever they promised. Like when someone promises you'll get Barbie for Christmas and you don't get Barbie for Christmas. Or when someone promises they'll drive you to the sixth-grade dance in the gym and they don't drive you anywhere. Now, I told John, I believe only in the promises of the Bible and in you. I suppose I was feeling light-headed from the loss of blood, because I blurted out, "Oh, John, John, John!"

The girls laughed. I turned around. They were all giving me the same look, *you sap*. Off by herself at the end of the pew, fast asleep, was Sherry. John stifled a yawn. "Who's next?"

I barely made it to the infirmary. When the nurse checked my pulse she saw two of my superficial cuts. When she rolled up my sleeve to take my blood pressure, she saw the serious artistic stuff. She made me lie down. She bought me a candy bar and sat on a chair beside my bed, with an expression of concern on her face, watching me eat it. At my request, she let me miss dinner and lie there all evening long, listening to the whippoorwills in the sycamore trees and reading back issues of *In Nature* magazine. There were a lot of fascinating-person stories in that magazine, things I could never dream up.

It was nice, having someone be kind to me. Her name was Nurse Woodham. I wish she hadn't said "like wood and ham" because she wasn't like wood or ham. She had soft, brown, curly hair and sad eyes. The skin across her cheeks and forehead was rough with little dents. She was pretty old to be a Miss, I guess. I thought she was kind and lovely and if I were a man, I would have married her, just for sitting beside me on that little white chair, keeping me company while I lied through my teeth. I told her my father was facing life imprisonment.

"What'd he do, hon?" Nurse Woodham asked without a trace of judgment. I wondered if her father had done time too. I didn't tell her that he was an embezzler. Neither Dad nor Mom wanted anyone to know until it came out in the paper. Irregularities had been discovered over a year ago by officers of the bank where Dad was head teller. At this point in the investigation, $500,000 was missing. Dad wasn't telling Mother whether he'd spent it all or was hoarding a part of it, because, he'd said, she would crack under the pressure of their questioning. I wish he'd told me. I wouldn't crack. He could trust me with any secret. I could tell any lie, big or small, with a completely straight face. He didn't know that or anything else about me. I told Nurse Woodham that Dad was going to jail for killing a man who tried to rape mother and me after pretending to read our electric meter.

Nurse Woodham just sat at my bedside, looking at me with her sad, lovely expression and smoothed the hair away from my forehead over and over again until I closed my eyes.

I woke up at four in the morning in the infirmary. I loved the infirmary. I was going to do whatever I had to do, say whatever I had to say to stay in the infirmary until camp was over. I turned on the lights. I loved the bluish cast of the overhead fluorescents, the cool, antiseptic, healing smells. I went through Nurse Woodham's pleasant little cabinets thoroughly. It was the usual—gauze, methylate, Neosporin, Desitin, Robitussin, Imodium A-D. I found a nursey-looking pair of scissors and used them to cut off my black socks. A two-inch-high swath of sock had knitted itself around each ankle right into the healing scabs. The only way I could remove the swath was to yank it out a quarter inch at a time. With each yank, up came the scab and the tender, newly forming tissue beneath. I was impressed with how much of me was attached to the sock. Blood poured down over my feet.

In the full-length mirror next to Nurse Woodham's official scale, I appeared to be up to my ankles in blood. I was fascinated. I took off all my clothes to see how I looked naked so far. There were gentle, curving slashes along the upper arms and forearms; the thighs were deeply gouged; the calves were fussed over—old scabs intersected with new ones in a kind of

blobby abstract pattern. There stood I, half-tortured, half-painted, my own original work of art. I was proud of myself.

Behind me, Nurse Woodham screamed. I didn't know she slept in the infirmary. I thought she'd gone home. "Why have you done this to yourself?" she screamed.

Where to start?

"Get in here this minute," she yanked me, ankles flowing blood, into the first aid room. She made me lie down. "You are sick, hon," she said as she wrapped my ankles in terry-cloth towels. "You must get help." I told her I'd been sent to Methodist Camp to get help. "Hon," she said. "*Hon*. This is beyond Methodists."

She dressed the ankle wounds with cool antibiotic cream. She wrapped each ankle around and around with a white ribbon of gauze. It was beautiful to watch. "Let me call your mother, hon," she said. "I think she better come pick you up."

"She moved," I said. "I don't know where."

"Let's just call and see," Nurse Woodham said, patronizing me. She dialed the Des Moines telephone number on my index card and got the same disconnect recording I'd gotten. Her expression was one of such total sorrow and concern that I realized I did need help. I felt abject despair. I was also completely earnest. I remembered the words in *Power for Living*—this was the only state that produced results.

"Nurse Woodham," I said urgently. "I must be alone to pray." She snatched up my Swiss Army knife and every other sharp thing in the room and left me alone, naked and scarred. I knelt down at the edge of the infirmary bed and lowered my head onto my folded hands. I felt like a fraud in that position. I ended up asking God to make John dump his wife and marry me. I tried another position, torso straight, chin raised to the ceiling, folded hands just below the chin. That too made me feel phony. What I wanted was a cigarette. I wanted to walk out into the night, smoking no-hands with a saucy face tilted up at the sky. I began to seriously doubt the validity of what I'd been reading in *Power for Living*.

Nurse Woodham released me from the infirmary the next afternoon to attend Belief class, provided I would return immediately afterwards. Sitting in the first row early, quietly praying as usual, my pulse quickened—I heard the crisp snap of John's leather soles as he walked up the chapel aisle. He bent over me. "Can I see you after class?" he whispered, words I'd been longing to hear, though I wondered why his tone was angry and critical.

John was in a fiery mood. He paced back and forth in front of us like an athlete warming up. "Which life is morally more responsible," he asked, "the life of a person who never breaks a commandment or the life of one who does?"

Many hands were raised. The girls were getting the hang of

John's beliefs. My hand was up too—I had a very good example. I wanted to tell about the time I broke a commandment and it did more good than harm. It happened when I was visiting my aunt out east on Block Island. She sent me out hunting for a goose to kill for dinner. I got the goose in the sight of the gun and I shot it, but when I ran up to it, I discovered that what I thought was a goose was an exotic black swan. I left the gun there on the beach, and carried the swan home, sobbing and sobbing. I knew the meaning of the commandment Thou Shalt Not Kill. My aunt and I both felt so remorseful that we undertook to establish a bird conservation organization, so this would not happen again.

I waved and waved my arm at John. I accompanied the waving with a series of loud, urgent oohs. "Ooh, ooh, ooh," I said, but John avoided me. He would not so much as look in my direction.

After class, John asked Sherry to wait for him outside—he needed to talk to me privately. She looked particularly lovely this afternoon in a yellow-knit halter top with tight white shorts. For her lipstick, she'd borrowed the counselor's Tiger Lily orange. Her toenails were painted with the same shade of orange polish. They looked cute as candy in her white leather sandals. I wanted to look like that. Would I ever? If only my faith were pure.

"Maureen," John said. Again the critical tone. I hoped this

was a new severe stage in our love. "Is there anything on your conscience?" John asked. "Anything you'd like to confess?"

My father was the embezzler, not me. John could read it for himself soon enough—it would be all over the *Des Moines Register*. I looked him straight in the eye and said, "No."

"Does *Seventeen* magazine ring a bell?" he demanded.

The Teresa story, the girl with one skirt and one blouse, hadn't actually happened to me. I'd elaborated on a short story I'd read in Sherry's magazine. I didn't think anyone but me read the short stories in *Seventeen*. "No," I said.

"You have an opportunity here, Maureen," John said. "Tell the truth. Make yourself right with God, for God is not something up there." He raised his arm and pointed to the chapel ceiling. His biceps flexed juicily. I could see his black armpit hair. I'd never been so close to such moral magnitude. I felt naked. I felt lost and alone. I felt like the freaky, lacerated, flat-chested savage I was, the thing that aroused in Nurse Woodham a scream of horror. I deeply needed John's healing touch. "No," John said, "God is here." He cupped his heart. John, John, John! Cup mine, I prayed.

"*Seventeen*," he said. "Does it ring a bell?"

"I don't know what you're talking about," I said.

"Perhaps, then, you know something about this," he said. He reached in his back pocket and pulled out my lost letter. It

was folded into a fat wad. I'd forgotten it was so long. I'd forgotten what exactly I said. It's possible some parts were too personal.

I took the letter, unfolded it, and turned to the last page, the one I feared the most. *I love you with a love that shames me. I shiver for you, I shake. I quiver for you, I quake.* I handed it back. "That's not my signature." It wasn't my signature. Whoever gave John my letter had signed my name.

Angrily, he stuffed it into the chest pocket of my blouse right over my heart. His knuckles brushed the place where my breast did eventually grow. Hadn't I just prayed *cup mine*? For once, my prayers were answered! At John's touch, I could almost feel the stored-up estrogen cascading forcefully into my breasts from wherever it had been hiding. It was like the Red Sea swallowing the Egyptians. For months, I could make myself weep, remembering the moment my prayers were answered as John's knuckles brushed me there. I could make my new best friend, Lynnette from Friendship, Arkansas, weep too. Friendship was the town Mom had picked out for our new start. Lynnette never got tired of hearing about my last sad night in Iowa when my handsome, thirty-year-old Greek boyfriend, John, said good-bye and gave my love letters back.

"Someone is trying to persecute me," I said. I got my shoul-

ders to convulse; I got real tears to pour down my cheeks; I got my nose to run. I expected him to comfort me physically, like the sympathetic shepherd that he was. When he didn't, I threw myself into his arms. It wasn't easy—I was nearly a head taller. He held me at arm's length.

"Maureen," he said, "please. Please, Maureen." His voice was impatient and annoyed. "Swear to me that you did not write that letter." He pointed at my breast. I swore. "Swear to me that you were not familiar with the contents of that magazine." He pointed to the pew where the girls in my bunk always sat. I swore. "Go," he said.

"I feel the need to pray," I said, staying put.

"Help yourself," he said and walked down the aisle, dabbing at the mucus I'd smeared on his shirt. As he opened the chapel door, I saw Sherry in her yellow halter waiting for him. What the other girls were saying about them, I didn't believe. John had restraint. John had self-control. I had proof. He could have taken advantage of me just now—I'd thrown myself at him. The chapel was empty. No one would have seen us. He could have done with me whatsoever he pleaseth.

Nurse Woodham was urgently expecting me, I knew, but I did need to pray. I kneeled on the steps of the nave. I wiped my nose on my sleeve. I folded my hands in prayer.

Silent Retreat

The ashram was the former estate of a robber baron who had made his fortune in railroads. The exterior of the mansion had been painted a hilarious, jumpy orange. It was a shade of orange that would do fine in a very hot, very spiritual country like India or Mexico, but here, under the gray, interdenominational skies of upstate New York, looked flimsy and Halloweenish.

REGISTRATION FOR SILENT RETREAT read a little sign. I followed the arrow into the kitchen where a beautiful, starved-looking girl in long white robes sat at a desk. "I'm Kali," she said. After I'd written out a check for the full amount, Kali said, "Please remove shoes." I did. She then said, "Now, your

room. Please follow." I felt very self-conscious and lummoxy, padding up the carpeted steps of the grand central staircase in not my newest pair of socks behind a girl in a sheet who had clearly been raised in a middle-class suburb somewhere and was now affecting Indian immigrant syntax.

"Your bed," Kali said, pointing to the narrowest of three in a large sunny room which, based on the huge, fanciful oak window seat had once been the nursery. I poked the mattress. I put my overnight kit on the nightstand. "Om Shanti," Kali said as she closed the door.

I sat down on the bed feeling fat and frowsy. I should have gone to a spa, I thought. To a hairdresser and a spa. If Peg and Sal could see me now. For a week, they'd tried to talk me out of this crazy adventure. They used the hygiene angle, saying the young people in places like this one shared combs, underwear and toothbrushes. They were convinced I'd get head lice. They are very dear, my two oldest friends, each in her own way. Peg lost a son in Vietnam, so she knows what I'm going through. Sal lost a fingernail in a restaurant so she *thinks* she does.

I'm here because nothing else has worked and I'm sick of being a bitter old nobody whose main claim to fame is that my only child is a vegetable. Alma, my daughter, attended Silent Retreat twice. She was driving up to number three when a

tractor-trailer hit her head-on. That was five years ago. Yes, five. And I visit her every day.

On my pillow is a typewritten schedule for the entire weekend, indicating meal times, meditation times, when to walk in the woods, when to rest. It is Friday, February 5 at 4:00. Time to rest. I try to. I try very hard. I set an example by lying very still with closed eyes even though two other female participants, my roommates, enter noisily, coughing, sniffling, unzipping duffel bags, banging hangers, dropping hairbrushes on the floor. I worry that this will ruin the retreat. These ashram people are serious and they know what they're doing. If they tell you to rest, it's because you need to rest. I would point this out to the ladies but how can I when we're all keeping silence?

The schedule calls for us to snack for an hour beginning at 6:15 P.M.—that's how I choose to interpret it. We gather in a high-ceilinged ballroom with sky-blue, deep-pile, wall-to-wall carpeting. Everyone else lowers themselves gracefully to the floor on folded legs. I land with a thud; my legs won't cross. Kali brings each of us one pear, six dates and a vitamin C. Consumption time: one minute. If Peg and Sal could see me now. *I'm hungry*, I write to Kali. "Light diet is best for silence," she says. "Keeps the mind alert." *I'm thirsty*, I write. She brings me, she brings us all, chamomile tea.

Swami Barami enters with his sitar in a playful custom-sewn calico case—made from the same calico print as my toaster cozy. With pain, I notice that he's aged since the days of the photo Alma keeps—kept?—in her meditation corner, although his hair is still black as kohl. His skin is beautifully clean and oiled and he smells like heaven. His irises are both dark and bright—I expected an earnest, ministerial look about the eyes, but his are aglow with mischief, as if the universe is run by a little joke. He removes the calico case and tunes the instrument at length. It's nothing but a vegetable, he giggles. All it is is a giant gourd, he says, a gourd that's carefully dried for ten years, then shellacked. Everything he says makes him laugh.

Before he plays, he thanks us for coming. He places his palms together in prayer and bows to us, touching the center of his forehead with his fingertips. His eyes close and the expression on his face is intense and courageous as his well-calloused fingers fly vigorously over the strings. The raga is a rain of ten million notes and not one of them falls on me. I spend all of Session One looking around the room, totally, but totally unimpressed by the other participants. Alma told me there were eight to twelve participants, men and women of all ages, and that a marvelous intimacy developed among them over the course of the three silent days, an intimacy that

caused them all to agree on Sunday evening when the silence was broken that had they talked their hearts out for three days, they could not have arrived at so deep a sensitivity and so natural a respect for one another.

What I see is losers. Everyone with an attitude. There's a big, unhealthy brooder, withdrawn and morose, sitting in the club chair with a ski hat pulled down over his ears. There's a married couple who are showing off their meditation style, matching salt and pepper shakers, backs straight, hands distorted in ashram sign language in their laps. There's a golden-haired youth just in from the West Coast, lying against the celestial blue of the carpet, his beautiful hands falling open, eternal as statuary. There's a snoopy young woman writing an article about this. Like me, she's looking around and she doesn't look impressed either, especially when she sees me, spying on her through ragged bangs, clasping and unclasping, clasping and unclasping my hands.

At night, someone snores. I'm sure it's her.

Just before morning, I dream of walking across a vast plain of mud. It is soft, slick, coffee-brown mud; a thin layer of it apparently covers the entire planet. I'm walking and walking. In the mud I see a fleck of gold. I kick at it. It gets longer. It's Alma's lost locket, I think in the dream, her little gold neck chain with the heart-shaped locket. I pick at it. I pull. It turns

into something that nips my wrist like a cat that doesn't like the way you're petting it. Then whatever-it-is evaporates.

Who am I? I wonder during our silent breakfast. Alma knew me as no one knew me. That's why I can't let her go. Letting Frank go was easy. He was just a man, a noisy, loyal man who liked to eat and hear me sing. When he died, I was sad, but I had Alma, I had Alma.

In Session Two we sit so long, it's physically painful. Session Three is worse. I sleep. Our silent walk which I've been looking forward to all morning is just as hard on my back and legs as the sitting. I spend Session Four looking at the others. All faces are strained, all backs looked pinched, all brains weak from fasting. Your instructions are simply to listen, Swami Barami giggles at the beginning of each session. I try to obey but Silent Retreat is not working on me. I decide to leave early. I have a return bus schedule in my purse. I will go to Snack, then sneak out and take the bus back.

We straggle separately across the grounds of the ashram to the lodge for Snack. A few hard clear constellations are maintained in the winter sky like tools in an arctic outpost. Inside the lodge, we fill our bowls. Soup—flavorful, pungent soup. I go back for more three times. The clinking of the steel spoon in the institutional tureen is harsh and hollow. The radiator sizzles. These sounds which should evoke comfort and shelter

echo instead with desolation, confirming the isolation each one of us feels. Single file we follow Swami Barami back to the ballroom.

He tunes the sitar. The brooder takes off his ski hat. The married couple sit on opposite sides of the room. The golden youth lies on the carpet with open hands but he looks less like statuary now, more like a man for whom the essence of things keeps slipping through his fingers. The writer and I have been competing each session to commandeer a huge, particularly soft pillow; this time she donates it to me. I'm grateful; I'm pooped. I plop down with a thud, then realize I've forgotten to sneak out.

At the sound of the first note, I feel an alertness in my bloodstream. The music is like a golden thread, helping me sit. I feel a sorrow that is rounded out by a bird's-eye overhead view of love. The raga is blazing away. I am the source of each one of the ten million notes. Hello Peg, Hello Sal, I think to myself, who's meditating now?

The next morning, Session Six is a snap. During Reflection, I wander into the library. I'm feeling confident; I go hog-wild; I read the *Kama Sutra*. I spend a few minutes hoping Alma never did any of this. Then I notice a position that Frank and I inadvertently held for ten minutes one evening when I knocked his glasses onto the floor. I reached down for his

glasses while we were still engaged and I almost had them when our houseguest knocked on the bedroom door asking for towels. I told the guest where the linen closet was. Then because the bathroom shared a very flimsy wall with our creaky iron bed, Frank and I hung fire in this unusual position with me half off the bed while the guest took a very quiet bath. Hello Peg, I'm thinking, hello Sal, look who's tantric!

Swami Barami brings the Silent Retreat to a close with a session of chanting, then we have a feast. There are flowers on the table in the lodge, and one big beautiful vegetable dish after another. We can talk now, but we don't feel like it. We smile at each other as we fill our plates. There are platters of gleaming fire-orange carrots, mounds of blue-green broccoli florets, lacy rounds of green and yellow squash looking as lively and intelligent as starfish, spicy red-pepper strips sautéed with toasted peanuts and garlic, stir-fried rice with ginger and scallions, a seven-grain bread so smart you could send it to college.

Swami Barami sits in the middle of us, wearing his favorite toy, a red plastic fireman's hat with a revolving, flashing red light on top. I admire it so passionately, he offers to let me try it. When I click on the battery-operated siren, the others applaud. I notice that Kali and Shakti and Shiva look a little left

out, eating at their quiet distant table. Unplug me, Alma says. In the morning, I tell her, *in the morning*. When I give Swami the hat back, I thank him *his* way, touching the center of my forehead with the fingertips of my praying hands.

Part Three

Me, Gus

Six months before, I'd have been a nut case—blurry vision, pressure in the chest. No more—I know what to do. I hum. In the Macy's elevator, I hum and between verses I take two, three deep breaths. I don't care who moves away from me. Only thing bad I do as I pass DIM SUM DEMONSTRATION is sweat, which I fixed already in Men's Cologne. Fucking Amazons bend in half to spray me.

In the demo classroom, I see my lovely lady, she has saved me a seat. Her head is narrower than I remember, her shoulder pads bigger. She's wearing a white angora thing with black leather sleeves, her necklace is a string of big gold balls. She sees me, she smiles. As I slip in beside her, I take the liberty of

caressing her wrist the way I caress the wrist of my wife, Holly, Holly of the Cheesecake, Holly of the Pound Cake, Holly of all the warm, evenly baked things I love when I am likewise late and slipping in beside her. "Lookin' good," I say to Sydney. "Lookin' good."

"Shh," says the lady in front of us. Sydney is sniffing the air. A number of ladies sitting around us are doing the same. I am very glad that I smell good.

"How you doin'?" I ask Sydney.

"Shh," says the lady in front again. I'm ready to tell her to get some fucking hair. She's got a bald spot the size of my palm, but Sydney points her rich little nose at the cook. Pay attention, Gus, she's telling me, so I do. I can be polite.

The cook is a tiny little Chink whose English is not too good. "Excuse me," the cook says, holding up a brown bottle. "Oyster sauce don't be stingy. Salt you can stingy. But not oyster sauce."

"Ah-so!" I say to Sydney. The lady in front gives me a look. *Oyster sauce*, Sydney writes in her loopy backhand, just the kind of handwriting you'd expect from a girl with three famous last names, one her father's, one her mother's, one the same as her ex. She's got her classy little purse notebook open on her lap. Mm, I'm looking at it, lap, lap, lap. *Pork fat*, she writes next, *bought or trimmed from a fresh ham*. Now you know

this girl is never going to trim fat from a fresh ham. This same notebook she had in Typography class. And she never did any Typography either.

"Now, shrimp," says the cook. She holds up a cleaver. "Chinese cook only use cleaver. Never knife. Cleaver does everything. Cleaver does work of all tools in kitchen. Only more fast." She dices a pound of shrimp in a minute. I cup my hands over my privates and elbow Sydney. She laughs.

"Shh." The lady in front of us says it to Sydney this time. Sydney sticks out her tongue. This girl loves me, I'm thinking, me, Gus, the guy who pastes up the Ho-Ho-Kus Shopper. This is something.

The cook is now crushing water chestnuts in her bare hand —the woman is a weapon. She mixes everything together, bang-bang, she's got dumplings. She steams them, she stirs up a sauce, and we're eating Chinese food. It's not brown and salty like real Chinese food, but Sydney likes it. She's even eating the rice. Let her fill up, that's the important thing. No way am I taking this girl out to dinner tonight, not after last week.

Last week, our first date, we're both very nervous. She tells me to pick a restaurant, so I pick Beefsteak Charlie's, then she says, "No, let's go to La Laguna." We go to La Laguna, she orders Veal Something, which she does not eat, I get the steak. The bill comes, it's eighty-eight bucks, she jumps up

and goes to the bathroom, I gotta pay. I'm smart—I remember my Loan-Yourself-a-Loan checks. They look like regular checks, but they allow you to borrow a hundred bucks with no record of where the money is spent. Once I drop that hundred, I make it clear I ain't going home without getting what I came in for if it takes all night, and it almost does. She keeps changing her mind. Six fucking months I worked on this girl. I ain't waiting another week.

So now when Sydney's little paper plate is empty I get her out of there, I get us a taxi and in the back, we're starting already. Mm, looks like she don't need her mind changed tonight. Thank you, Saint Anthony, I'm thinking. Thank you, Saint Christopher. All of you who got me here with her tonight, thank you, thank you.

Know what my favorite part is? My favorite part is the look on her face when I'm stuffing her. First she looks like she's trying to climb backwards up a ladder to get out of the way of this *thing*. Then she looks like this thing is starting to fit. And then she sinks down onto it, like it's a missing piece of her she's found and never wants to lose again.

Me, I got time to walk to Port Authority for the 12:20 bus. Never have a better trip through that tunnel—I sleep all the way. The driver wakes me up at Ho-Ho-Kus, I walk up Weber Street to my house. Slipping into bed beside Miss Fat Ass at 1:24 A.M. I am one happy man.

I'm still happy in the morning, I'm congratulating myself as I get dressed, I'm not even tired. Then I can't find my wallet. Fucking wallet is gone. I've been pickpocketed somewhere in that lousy, filthy city, after I bought my ticket, probably at the gate where I nodded off, waiting for the 12:20.

I got no choice, I write myself another Loan-Yourself-a-Loan check to get through until payday. Now, what am I going to tell Holly, Holly who is smarter than me, Holly who believes me when I say I'm in the city to see Heywood about a freelance job? Holly pays the bills and does the checkbook. She goes through our charge slips like Columbo. She don't want me taking nobody, man or woman, out to eat because I won't take her out to eat. I tell her she's too fat already. One of the hundreds I could say was a pickpocket, but not both. How long do I have until she gets the bank statement in the mail? A week, ten days. Then I'm in deep shit.

Sydney, meanwhile, starts calling me at the office every day. Mrs. Wharton from Bloomingdale's is how she identifies herself to the receptionist. She wants to take me to the World Trade Center for drinks. She wants to rent a hotel suite. She wants us to go to Barbados. I tell her I got deadlines. Which is true. I got *the* biggest freelance deadline of my life—my future depends on it. She don't let up.

"Please, Gustav," she says, and the guy at the drawing board in front of me, Hal, he picks up on my line by mistake and

hears Sydney saying to me, "Let me come to Jersey, I can't wait another week." Hal looks over his shoulder at me, grinning, he's impressed. I give him the thumbs-up sign. I would shoot myself through the head before I would give this girl directions to Ho-Ho-Kus. But Hal don't need to know that.

So the ten days go by, no mention from Holly of the two hundred bucks. I know she knows because when she's taking her morning shit, I look at the bank statement which is right there on her desk with the two amounts circled. Meanwhile, she is cooking up a storm, all the things I love, baked ziti, the pork pastries with the onions and sausage inside, homemade cannoli and cheesecake. Holly makes the best cheesecake you ever tasted. Plus, she is shutting up.

I ain't used to this.

I have seen a number of ladies. Two times before, when Holly became suspicious of me, she started following me around everywhere. If I said I was working late, she would show up at the Shopper, she would talk. About what, I can't remember, but she would talk, talk, talk. If I said I was going out for a little drive, she would come along. Same thing, talk, talk, talk. I would stop seeing this certain someone more or less to get Holly off my back, to get her to stop following me around and shut the fuck up.

This time, she is shutting up. Holy shit, I'm thinking, she

sees me making something of myself, she sees me taking the bus through the tunnel, every week, no problem. She's afraid that I'm going to leave her now that I can get through the tunnel.

See, this whole thing goes back to the tunnel.

Pop brought us up hating the city, wanting nothing to do with it. It's a filthy, lousy place he told us, and they can have it. We believed him and we never went near the place. But after I married Holly—do you believe it, she weighed one-twenty on our wedding day—she wanted to go there. She'd never been to a Broadway play. So I'm the man, I'm going to take her to her first musical. We get dressed up, we drive down Route 17 to 3, traffic is a little heavy, but we got plenty of time. Bang, bang, we get to the ramp, there's a major backup. Now this happens to be my first time on the ramp. This ramp is very steep and it curves down like a big chute that empties you right into the tunnel. When I see the setup, I start to have problems. I can't go inside this tunnel. This is a very deep river, the Hudson, very deep. The water is filled with live eels, dead bass, pieces of bodies, factory sewage, human crap, you name it. And all of these vehicles—we are bumper-to-bumper in eight, ten, twelve lanes of traffic—are forced to merge into one little tiny two-lane tunnel. And what I don't know is does this tunnel go under the ground that's

under the river or is it in the river? Because if it's in the river and you're in it when the tunnel snaps in two, you get the worst of every possible death combined. You die under water in your car with tractor-trailers and buses smashing into you. You're crumpling and sinking and filling with water very, very slowly. You can't open your door because the water pressure is too great. And if you could open it, you'd be in a tunnel.

No way am I going to die like that.

I'm suffocating already, my vision is blurry, the pressure in my chest is making it hard to breathe. This reminds me, don't ask me why, of when I'm being operated on when I'm a kid and they give me ether. It feels like green death closing in. They say they're going to stunt the growth in my right leg so the left leg can catch up, so one leg won't be longer and I can wear shoes with regular soles. Anyway, I think I'm dying again now. I start to back the car up the ramp. I back up an inch here, an inch there. Everybody is honking, everybody is cursing.

"What's wrong with you?" Holly is yelling. I don't answer. Guys are getting out of their trucks to beat me up. I lock the doors. I give them the finger. And I keep on backing up, inch by inch, across all these lanes of cars and trucks, buses and vans, trying to get over to the right-hand shoulder of the ramp. Holly is so embarrassed she climbs in the back and lays

down flat on the seat trying to hide. One hour it takes to get that car, all four wheels, completely on the shoulder. Then I can go much faster, a couple miles an hour, right back up the ramp to the Weehawken exit. I turn around. We go home. I tell Holly, "If you ever, *ever* tell Pop about this, or anybody else, I will break every bone in your body." One week we were married. I should have said it nicer.

Make a long story short, ten years go by, we never go through that tunnel. Once we go to a wake on Staten Island. We leave plenty of time and take the bridge, which I am not too fond of either, and the ferry. Holly never tells nobody about my problem. She's a good wife except she turns my kids against me, but every wife does that. What else can they do, sitting home all day with nothing to look forward to? It makes them feel they've accomplished something if the kids take their side on everything. So there we are, Georgie is eight, Kimmie is six, we live up the street from Ma and Pop, across from my brother, Freddie, and his wife, Janie, same house for ten years. I still have my same job, pasting up the Shopper, I got my lovely ladies on the side to keep things interesting. I am discreet, more discreet than Pop ever was—only two times out of the eight does Holly suspect.

Now something starts to bother me. I have not made anything of myself and at this rate, I ain't going to. The only peo-

ple who think highly of me are these girls. They see me walk down the street and they see the high point of their week. They see an artist. More than one has used that word. But what does your average person see? Me, Gus, a nobody, a guy with hairy arms who stands four foot eleven.

This gets me thinking about Joe Burns. Joe Burns made something of himself. He started in the Art Department when I started. Only he stunk. And he knew it. So he goes into the city at night and studies Business Administration. Bang, bang, he gets promoted. Now he makes two times what I make, he puts a kid through Rutgers.

So even though it seems too late to start, I'm thinking, better late than never. I got to know—how good am I? I know I'm good enough to take over the Art Department at the Shopper when Ford Logo croaks. This guy, I call him Ford Logo behind his back, because he gives every advertiser the Ford Motor logo, script in an oval. But am I good enough to go out on my own, start a little design studio, work with interesting people?

I send for information. Every night school, every art school, every adult education program in New York City is sending me catalogues. I read, I read. But I don't know where to start. And in the back of my mind, I know I got to go through the tunnel to get where I want to go. The bus goes

through the tunnel and I got to take the bus. I can't leave Holly alone with the kids without a car. So here I am, trying to decide, should I try illustration, should I try design, should I develop skills in the concepts of advertising?

Bang, there it is, the answer: Introduction to Typography with Heywood Jarrell. I have always had a fascination with letters. Freddie used to say I was nuts, I would draw the alphabet as many ways as I could think of when we were little. I drew script. I drew letters with shading. Heywood Jarrell, it says in the Instructors Notes, revolutionized the marketing of panty hose with the introduction of the egg-shaped container into the supermarket segment. Holy shit, I missed the joke all these years, eggs and legs. The man is a genius. I sign up. But I don't tell nobody. Why? Because how do I know if I can make it through the tunnel?

So at the Labor Day barbecue—every Labor Day we have a big barbecue in Pop's backyard—Holly does it, she betrays me. In front of all of them, she starts yelling, "Hey, everybody, Gus is going big time." I'm standing there eating a huge plate of Ma's scungilli salad, the kind I like with the olive oil and the garlic. Everybody is looking at me. "Gus is going into the city nights. He's going to study art." I am anxious to know how she found this out. Nobody is reacting yet because they don't know if this is a joke or what.

"Whoa!" Pop says. He puts down the tongs—he's grilling sausages—and he looks at me the way he used to when he wanted to beat the pants off me at pool. "Going into the city to study art!" Everybody starts to smile—they're all deciding it's okay to make fun. "Taking the big step, Gus?" Pop says. "You're going to show them, right? You're going to be big time, right? You, Gus from Ho-Ho-Kus."

Now everybody is having fun. Even Ma. Nobody is sticking up for me. Holly's on a roll. "And guess how he filled out the application?" she yells. "He put his name as GUSTAV." I'm thinking about how her nose will look after I mash it straight up into her forehead.

"Gus*tav*," Janie says, and she sticks her nose up in the air, "Are you still going to speak to us?"

"What kind of name is Gustav," Freddie says, "Russian? Because somehow you don't look Russian. I never seen a Russian five feet tall."

"Low blow," Janie says, but everybody is laughing. Now each of these people has told me privately that I am wasting myself professionally at the Shopper. Each one has told me I have talent. Yet now that I'm doing something about it, they're making fun of me. And yet, what have they done that entitles them to ridicule me like this? Everybody here is worse off than they were a year ago. Pop's gut is hanging another

inch over his belt, Mom's got another hair on her chin, Holly's got another chin, Freddie's another grand in debt from gambling, Janie's taking two kinds of tranquilizers instead of one.

Georgie and Kimmie are both looking at me, and for once they are on my side. Both faces are saying the same thing: do something, Dad. Make them stop. So I do. First I put down my plate. "Hey," I say. "Hey, know what?" And Holly gets that look on her face like she's afraid of what I might do next. I point to each one of them in turn and I say, "Fuck you, Dad. Fuck you, Fred. Fuck you, Holly and you, Jane. Not you, Ma. And not you, kids." And I leave. I walk out of the backyard, down the street to my house and I get in my car and start driving. And when I'm driving, I'm thinking, what if Pop is right? What if I'm full of shit? What if I can't do as well as the young kids of today? What if I can't even get through the tunnel to find out? What then?

The first night of class is September 13. I will never forget that day. I get butterflies in my stomach after lunch. I tell Ford Logo I'm going home sick, thinking I'll get into the city early, miss the rush. A big mistake. Every person on the 3:20 has problems, that's why they're on the 3:20. If they fit into society, they would be somewhere else, at work, at home. In back we got a bum drinking out of a brown paper bag. In the middle we got a fat lady who stinks like anchovy paste. In front we

got a mumbler. I sit behind the driver, so I can talk to him if I get the attack in the tunnel. Two girls with a radio get on at the next stop and sit right behind me, listening to salsa and chewing grape gum. The mumbler is mumbling into his hands. Every now and then he looks at me and says, "The cuckoo clocks are going to make the fat people pay." That's what he says, "The cuckoo clocks are going to make the fat people pay." Now what does that mean to you, because it don't mean nothing to me. It almost means something, but you think about it and bang, it means nothing.

I'm okay until we start down that ramp. What is it about that ramp? It's steep, it curves down, I feel like I'm in a chute and I'm rolling down to be slaughtered. I get the blurry vision, the pressure in the chest, I can't breathe. I'm sweating like a pig, straight through my jacket. I start a conversation with the driver when he stops at the tollbooth to pay, but he can't hear me because, turns out, he's deaf in the right ear. I put my head between my legs, close my eyes, hold tight to my Saint Christopher medal. Over and over, I'm saying, Just get me over, Saint Christopher. The bus is going downhill, down, down, and when the sound changes, no traffic noise, just wheels, I know we're in the tunnel. The smell of exhaust is seeping in underneath somewhere. The bum in back is smoking a cigarette. Green death is closing in around me. This is it,

I'm thinking, this is the end. Just get me over, I'm praying, I probably say it two thousand times.

Then we're in the light. I can sit up. When I look out, we're swinging up into the entrance to Port Authority. Thank you, Saint Christopher, I'm saying. I stand up too fast, I got to get off that bus, I faint. I cut my head on the metal fare box. The driver is slapping my face, wiping my head with his handkerchief. He puts me on the escalator. When I'm on the street on solid concrete, alive and breathing, it's like I'm having a religious experience. I know that everyone around me is rushing and running and there's tremendous noise, but to me, they're moving in slow motion. Everything is peaceful and glowing. Especially the women. The women crossing the street, standing in line, paying for things, swinging briefcases, they are all beautiful. I've never seen so many colors, sizes, shapes and kinds. More tits, hair, legs and lips than I could sample in a lifetime. Jerks, I'm thinking of Pop and Fred, jerks in Jersey, sitting in a lawn chair looking at the back of a 7-Eleven, saying New York stinks!

On the corner is a hot-dog cart. I have two with everything, sauerkraut, onions, relish, mustard. These two hot dogs are the best hot dogs I ever ate.

I get to the school an hour and a half early, and I spend a little time talking to the janitor to get the lay of the land. He

unlocks the classroom for me. I'm the first to meet Heywood. Heywood Jarrell is English. He's got curly red hair. He wears a red bow tie with a purple sweater vest. Later, when I buy a vest just like it, I buy green, so I don't copy him. I tell Heywood I think he is dynamic, a great genius of the field. He seems pleased. "And you are?" he asks.

"Gustav Angellini."

I help set up the slide projector.

When it's time to start, Heywood calls the roll, beginning with me. "Mr. Angellini," he says and nods in my direction, and I say, "Yo." Just like that, nothing loud, nothing show-off. "Yo," I say, just like that. Every kid in this class laughs. "Yo." What is so funny about that? These kids are rich kids, Jewish kids, we got Steins, we got Bergs, we got Kleins. Every lawyer, every accountant, every doctor you ever heard of has a kid in this class. They all got fancy pens and fancy pads and they doodle all the time and they slouch. They got their legs up on other chairs. This was not allowed when I was in school.

The last name in on the roll, Sydney Dunbar Wharton, doesn't answer. Heywood calls it three times, but there's no answer. He turns out the lights. He shows us slides of the one hundred finest examples of packaging in the history of American advertising. In each case, he shows us the major role of

typography in the impact. Some of the impact I have noticed on my own all these years—I pride myself on this.

Heywood's halfway through when the door opens and in comes someone who sits down next to me. She smells like red roses and expensive wool and fingernail polish. This smell becomes deeply embedded in my learning process. When Heywood turns on the lights again, I'm in love. Turns out, I'm in love with Sydney Dunbar Wharton.

After class, I try to make conversation with this girl. She's wearing a red knit dress with big shoulder pads and a gold zigzag down the front. She's too tiny for this look—she looks like she opened Wonder Woman's closet by mistake. I ask her if she wants to have a cup of coffee with me, maybe a sandwich. "You've got to be kidding," she says.

This does not discourage me. More than one of those eight girls started out believing I was a joke. No woman pictures her knight in shining armor as short. But when all is said and done, believe me, the joke is not on me.

"Maybe next time," I say. Sitting by the gate in Port Authority waiting for the 10:10, I try to concentrate on Heywood's first assignment, which is to study the type book and pick out any style of lowercase letter that resembles an animal. I think I got one or two. The bus comes, I start to sweat. I got to get through that tunnel without fainting or I might give up, I

might not come back. I can't breathe, I'm suffocating. Filthy yellow-green tile is all around us, we're trapped inside, the air is filled with gas, and we're going deeper. I got to come up with something. I take a couple deep breaths, and I try humming. Two people get up and move as far away from me as they can. I don't care. I ain't letting nothing stop me if I can help it. Bingo, the humming works. I concentrate completely on the humming. The humming makes it possible.

Hours I spend on that assignment, all weekend I am studying that type book. Holly is surprised. She is even more surprised when Wednesday rolls around and I go back to class. She is expecting me to make an excuse and stay home. P.S., Heywood loves what I have done. He loves my animals. I got an *a* that looks like a profile of a deer, a seahorse which is a *c* turned around, a snail on its side made from a *d*. The only kid who comes close to me is the Klein kid with the army jacket who brings in an owl face, an upside-down *m*.

Sydney makes a complete fool of herself. Sydney does exactly what Heywood said not to do when he gave us the assignment. "Do not," he said, "bring in any *s* that looks like a snake. I never want to see another *s* that looks like a snake as long as I live." And there she is with the worst *s* you could imagine, looking just like a snake. Heywood screams like he is seeing a mouse—and the man is not a faggot. "Who did that?" he says.

She cries and runs out of the room. I go after her. She is standing on the curb waving down a taxi when I catch up. I get out a piece of bristol board. GUSTAV, I draw in Frankfurter Bold, then I draw the phone number of the Shopper. In the corner, I sketch a cartoon of my face on a short body. Fair is fair. I give this to her as she is getting inside the taxi. "Call me if you want help with the homework," I say. "I got more than enough ideas."

She don't call. The next week she comes in with more terrible homework. We're supposed to select capital letters with interesting negative space. What does she bring in? A big, circusy *A* with curls and flourishes.

"No," Heywood says in a voice like he is training a puppy dog. "No, no, no. You are striving for shape instead of striving for impact. First, look at the edge where white meets black, then focus on the white space alone. What is the form? Where is the weight?"

Might I add that the most commented-on piece was my sideways *H*? "It's sexy," Heywood says. "There's great surface tension. It jumps. Sometimes you see the *H* and sometimes you see the cleavage." The guy has a way with words.

We miss one class. Heywood has to travel someplace to receive an award, so he gives us a hard assignment which should take two full weeks to complete: a portrait composed only of lowercase letters typed on the typewriter. I am the

star. Two weekends I spend at the Shopper, working on this piece, a portrait of Sydney. The hair I do with *c*'s and *t*'s. The shadows in the face I do with *i*'s. The body I do with *x*'s, except for certain lovely areas of interest which are *o*'s. The knees and ankles and high heels are little *k*'s and *j*'s. I'm gone so long Holly is suspicious. She follows me down to the Shopper, she watches over my shoulder, she asks me what it's a picture of. I say it's abstract. She gives me the look with the chins. She tucks in all her chins and looks at me out of the corner of one eye, same look she gives the kids when they tell her only two of the three places they've been.

This piece knocks Heywood out. "This is it," he says to all the kids. "This is what I want to see, what Mr. Angellini has done. All of you, take note, please."

This time when I invite Sydney for a cup of coffee, she comes. She orders Sanka with Sweet'n Low, Half & Half on the side. This girl is working way too hard to get what she wants out of a cup of coffee. "I'm not going back," she says. "I don't get typography." This time I agree with her. Her portrait consisted of the typewritten words ELIZABETH TAYLOR over and over. She didn't want Typography in the first place, she tells me, she only took Heywood's class because Photography was full. She says she's just divorced—her shrink told her to take a class in something to meet people. "Hey," I say, "we have

something in common. I took a class to meet people too. And I met you."

"I don't think he meant for me to meet you, though," she says.

"Ask him," I say.

Make a long story short, she never comes back to Typography. I can't stand this. I got to have this girl, I got to know what she's like. I pull a stat of the portrait of Sydney and mail it to her with a note, *This is you*. Hal sees me taping up the envelope in the mail room. "Who do you know at 50 Sutton Place?" he asks. "A millionaire?"

"Millionairess."

"Fucking guy has all the luck," Hal says.

Classic. That is the word Heywood uses to describe my next assignment which features a lowercase *g* I design myself. Turns out the lowercase *g* is Heywood's favorite letter.

By December, Heywood is telling me to come in and see him at his design studio. He's got freelance jobs for me. I go, we talk, he gives me a couple little logos, nonprofit jobs that don't pay much. I work, I work, I work on those jobs. He loves what I do. He gives me a bigger job, one that pays. I call Sydney from a pay phone on the corner. "Remember me?" I say. "I'm working for Heywood now."

She says she's frustrated. She's taking a seminar in book-

binding and everybody else is further along in the art than she is. I tell her I'm in the city all the time these days, if she wants help binding her books or feels like having a glass of wine. She groans. "I don't think so," she says.

For Christmas I draw her a beautiful little SDW, elegant but restrained, confined in a circle except for one serif on the *S* and one serif on the *W* which push out of the circle as if they can't stand it in there one second longer.

I don't hear nothing. Not a simple thank you. I give up. I give up on Sydney Dunbar Wharton, red roses, expensive wool and fingernail polish.

Weeks go by. I'm working night and day on my biggest Heywood job ever, the redesign from cover to cover of the graphics of a magazine for kids, affluent, urban kids from eight to eleven years old. One Tuesday I come back to the Shopper from a very big lunch and there it is, the pink slip I've been waiting for six months: *Mrs. Wharton called. Please call back.*

I call, we talk. She's finally happy. She's found a class she likes. It's Chinese Cooking. She likes it because you learn by watching, you don't have to do anything. She wants to see me.

I tell Holly I'm going in to meet with Heywood. She wants to know why I run home from work to take a shower before meeting Heywood when I never took a shower before meet-

ing Heywood before. “Mind your own business,” I say, and she gives me the look with the chins. I go in, I meet Sydney, we eat at La Laguna, I drop the hundred, you know the rest.

So. Holly is cooking everything I love, keeping her mouth shut about the two hundred. Sydney is calling me every day. She wants to take me to the World Trade Center for drinks. She wants to rent a hotel suite. She wants us to go to Barbados. Did I say that already? And I have to tell her I can’t, I’m too busy, I got deadlines. Which is true. I am redesigning a magazine for Heywood—me, Gus. I have everything I want all at the same time.

The problem is time. Having what you want takes time, more time than you might think when you don’t got shit. The next week, when I go in to deliver the biggie to Heywood, I try to see Sydney first. She’s late, I do her quickly, too quickly, she’s mad, she wants to talk. I’m nervous, I’m late for Heywood. He’s rushed—he has to leave without going over my stuff. I leave the job there and run back up to Sydney’s. She’s gone. I’m exhausted. On the bus going home, in the tunnel, I panic. I’m sweating, I’m suffocating, I’m humming and the humming don’t work. I’m scared to death, as scared as a little baby in his worst nightmare.

I get home. My night is not over. Miss Fat Ass is snoring away with the bedroom light on, all decked out in a new

orange negligee. There's an empty container of ice cream on the nightstand, the spoon is still in her hand. She fell asleep waiting for me. She looks ridiculous, like a baby whale in orange lace, but if I don't wake her up and stick it to her, she'll suspect something, so I do.

Next day, I can't get out of bed. Thank God, I got the Hong Kong flu. Two weeks I'm in bed, I don't go to work, I don't go to the city. Holly takes good care of me. She floats up like a big fat angel with a floral arrangement from Heywood. P.S. He loves what I did. I notice when I'm delirious I get many interesting type ideas. I play around with them. The house is quiet except for Holly's Mixmaster. I feel peaceful. I like delirium. If it were illegal, everybody would like it.

First day back at work, the receptionist gives me eighty-six messages from Sydney. I call her. Where was I? I was sick. Why didn't I call her? I was home—I was under twenty-four-hour watch by Holly. When can she see me? She can't. I'm busy, I say, I got deadlines. This time it's a lie. Bang, she goes nuts, she turns on me. "This is not working out," she says. "We're very different people with very different belief systems," she says. I listen to this.

"If that's how you feel," I say, "Fine. Go fuck yourself." I hang up. She calls back.

"You're incapable of intimacy," she says. Because I agreed

with her that it wasn't working out, she calls me incapable of intimacy. She says, "You're emotionally stunted and it makes you hostile to women." Turns out the only way I can prove to her that I'm not hostile to women is to finalize my separation. Perhaps I mentioned something early on about things not working out with Holly.

"Wouldn't that be hostile to Holly?" I ask. "If I separate?"

For this Sydney has no answer. I tell her Holly may have something wrong with her health, a brain tumor, and this is not a wise time to leave her. Sydney says she herself could easily develop breast cancer, it runs in her family, it's brought on by stress. The girl is nuts. She will not get off the phone. I tell her I got work to do and I hang up. The receptionist I order to hold my calls. By the end of the day, there's a stack of pink slips, Mrs. Wharton from Bloomingdale's, Mrs. Wharton from Bloomingdale's.

The truth is, I don't want to see her again and it's not because she's nuts. Nuts don't bother me. It's not even the two hundred she cost me, though that is a high average, a hundred bucks a pop. It's that my curiosity has been satisfied. See, most girls I only really need to stuff two times, the first time to put an end to the waiting, and the second time to relive the first. I know, I know, it ain't fair, but the truth is not often fair.

That night, I get home from the Shopper, something is dif-

ferent. The kids have eaten already, they're watching TV. Holly has made for me a big, rich, very special dish, seafood with linguine. She is opening a bottle of wine. The phone starts ringing. It rings eight, ten times. She don't answer it. She pours the wine and sits down. "Answer the fucking phone," I yell.

"You answer it, Gus," she says. "When I answer it, they hang up. All day they've been calling and hanging up. They've been calling everybody, Ma, Pa, Freddie, Janie, your cousins. Everybody knows."

"Knows what?"

She don't say nothing. I sit down and eat that whole platter of seafood with linguine. She eats two strings. I drink most of the bottle of wine. She drinks half a glass. Every time that phone starts ringing, she just looks at me over the rim of the glass and takes a sip. She don't say nothing. She is one unhappy girl.

She is doing the dishes when Freddie comes to the back door.

"Hey, Gus," he says, "why don't you answer the phone. I been trying to call you."

"That calling is you?"

"What calling?"

"Somebody's been calling all day and all night."

"That's why I was calling you," he says. "Somebody's been calling us too. Somebody's been calling everybody in the family and telling us about things you're doing in the city, Gus." Freddie, he winks. "You've been busy."

"Somebody's been calling Pop too?" I ask.

"Pop is this minute bragging about you down at Tony's. I just came from there."

"Bragging," I say. "About me. Now."

"Bragging. About you. Now."

"Because of the art I'm doing."

"Art? What art? Get out of here. The girl, Gus, the girl. Sutton Place—way to go!"

I ask Fred to tell me what Pop said, the exact words, so I can enjoy it, that he's proud of me, Gus. "No shit!" I say. Two, three times, I make him tell me.

Fred leaves. The phone starts ringing. I walk into the bedroom to answer it, Holly's in bed already, she's lying there wide awake without moving. She watches me pick up the phone. "Hello?" I say.

"Gus, my God, I have to see you." Sydney is crying. "I have to. I'm leaving now. I've talked to every Angellini in Ho-Ho-Kus and they know about us. Your wife is not sick. You're not getting away, Gus. I'm coming over to see you now. We have to talk."

"Listen, you," I say. "You call this number again and I'll mash your nose straight up into your head. I'll break every fucking bone in your body. The police are tracing this call, you understand, you fuck?" I slam down the phone. "It's a crank," I tell Holly. I call the police right in front of her and report the crank calls. I unplug the phone. "Night, Holl," I say. I sit in my BarcaLounger watching out the picture window in case Sydney does decide to come over here and get her nose mashed in. Do you know what it feels like to be sitting in a lounge chair as a grown man and still not have your fucking feet touch the floor? I fall asleep in my chair in my clothes, shoes, belt, everything. Two in the morning, I wake up, I'm cold. I make some cocoa, which is too hot, I burn the roof of my mouth. I put the fucking cup down, get a blanket, fall asleep in the chair again, wake up at five. I drink the cold cocoa.

I'm looking out the window at my street, it's getting light, I'm thinking. One more job from Heywood and I quit the Shopper. I'm thinking how nice that will be, not to ever go into that place again. I'm thinking along these lines, I hear a little rustling sound, I turn around. Standing there in the kitchen in her yellow robe looking at me over the rim of her teacup while she takes a sip is Holly. She's finally done it, Miss Fat Ass, she's got my respect, shutting up like that, very smart. See, certain things about me she never understood. I am

good. I am fast, I am good, and I ain't the type to burn out. Me, Gus, I got ideas, I got zillions of them. Turns out, all these years, I been saving up ideas without even knowing what I was doing.

Normal

Rae watched through the yellow calico curtains. He was shorter than she remembered, but his walk was the same, cocky. He still looked like a Sears model, clean, trim. Still dressed like one too, khaki slacks, madras shirt. She watched her father walk up the driveway to the wrong door.

She had told him to go around to the back of the big old house and climb the rear flight of stairs—their door was at the top. "I'll find it," he had said. He was rushing to get off the phone. He hadn't talked to her in five years, hadn't seen her since he kicked her out of the house when she was sixteen for doing drugs. He hadn't meant for her to leave Seattle, but that's what she did, she and her boyfriend, Jimmie. Jimmie

was dead now. Rae was married to Jimmie's best friend, Chris. They lived in upstate New York on a country road near the town of Hart Springs. Chris was a leader at the Seventh Day Adventist Retreat Center.

Rae rocked the baby in her arms. Her father was ringing the doorbell for the ground floor apartment. "He's waking up the old man," she told Chris. Chris was sitting on the sofa, staring into space. He was exhausted, stressed out over what he'd had to do. He'd been up all night doing it and now it was done. His brother was in a mental institution. It had been stressful for Rae too. For the first time since her son was born six weeks ago, Rae lost her milk. The baby kept trying to nurse, but was getting nothing. He tried again now. She slipped the bottle between his lips. The unfamiliar feel and smell of the rubber nipple made him furious. His forehead wrinkled into rows of tiny, unhappy folds. He thrashed his head from side to side, arching his back, releasing a loud cry. Rae rose up on one toe and spun around. Motion distracted him. She was praying—her version, not Chris's—that her milk would come back. The La Leche League advisor said to help it along, Rae should rest, rest, rest. Rae couldn't do that—her father was coming. She fluffed her son's fine black hair so it stuck straight up, just like hers.

She watched the old man lean out his window and point her

father in the right direction. Then, she lost sight of him. When she heard his footsteps on the wooden stairs, her pulse quickened. She was exhausted. She was insecure and apprehensive. He would think she looked unmaternal in her black sweater, black leather mini, black knee-high suede boots. She liked black. She'd always liked black. For years, it was the only color she would wear; now it was simply her favorite. She hoped he would notice that she'd made a home of the gabled attic apartment, though certainly not as much of a home as her mother was capable of making and remaking. Her mother decorated compulsively.

Rae had stayed up late the night before, installing the yellow calico curtains for her father's visit. The first time around, she screwed the rod holders into the sash backwards. A reasonable person would have stopped, put the tools away for the night and gone to bed—especially since she was supposed to rest to get back her milk. But Rae kept going. It was a necessity to have curtains up. Her father only had a few hours to spend. Curtains would hide the window with the broken glass. Curtains would soften the room in the homey way he was used to. Rae wept as she screwed the rod holders into the sash, correctly the second time, because it was so obvious. As nasty as he'd been to her, she cared what he thought.

Her father rang their bell. "Here we go," Rae said to Chris.

Chris roused himself from the sofa. He walked stiffly to the door—he'd hurt his shoulder wrestling with his brother. He arrived home from that obligation just in time to shower, shave, and put on a clean shirt for this one. Chris was tall with long legs and long, brown hair. He had the American Jesus look, West Coast style. His dark brown eyes, which used to look so selfish and dangerous, were deep and steady now. He opened the door.

"Norman," Chris said.

"Chris," he said. He was taken aback by Chris's height. Her father tilted back awkwardly, as if to say, no one prepared me, and gave Chris's extended hand a single, brief shake.

Chris smiled one of his enigmatic smiles—it wasn't clear to Rae if he liked what he saw or forgave what he saw. "Welcome," Chris said. With a sweeping gesture, he offered Norman the entire room to inspect, enjoy, take over.

Across the floor, Rae stood, nervous about the black, holding the baby.

"My man!" Norman crowed. His face lit up in a bright, joyous mask. He'd recovered his confidence. "There's the man I came to see!" The man. Did that mean the woman holding the man was not worth the trip?

As Norman lifted the baby out of Rae's arms, his fingers grazed hers. Rae was hoping for more touch. Her son was the

one who was getting it. She watched him to see if he liked it. Usually when a stranger tried to hold him, he screamed and writhed and reached back for his mother. But now he behaved. Perhaps he was stunned by Norman's bright mask-face and gung ho Seattle accent. "Way to go, partner," Norman said, waltzing the baby around the room. "Lookin' good."

"Nice to see you, Dad," Rae said in a flat voice meant to inform Chris playfully that she'd been rejected. Chris missed it. He was spacing out again. He had drifted over to the curtained windows and stationed himself in front of the one he knew was broken, broken by his brother.

His brother had shown up three days earlier without warning, always a bad sign. He had an important discovery to share with Chris: the dog they had when they were little was really their Uncle Norris and Uncle Norris was really half-Japanese. He told Chris he used to talk to Uncle Norris. Because they were talking half-Japanese, he never learned full Japanese. So now when he talked, everyone thought he was crazy.

Chris had, once before, committed his brother to a mental institution. He never wanted to do that again—his brother had gotten worse inside, not better. Chris wondered if his brother could be healed through prayer. He brought him to the center. The Adventists prayed over Chris's brother for two days, but Jesus did not come into his heart. In fact, his brother

bothered people. He was asked to leave the center. Chris brought his brother home.

Rae and the baby were out, shopping for curtains to warm up the place for her father's visit. He had lengthened a business trip to New York City by one day so he could see his grandson. Rae couldn't believe her parents were acting normal, responding to a birth announcement with a congratulatory phone call, sending gifts, coming to visit at the first available opportunity. In the past, they'd indicated Rae did not deserve the normal niceties. They'd seen some talk show on tough love, and the next time they found Rae and Jimmie stoned, they kicked them out. They got the tough part right, just forgot about the love.

When Rae came home from the store with curtains, Chris was back at the Adventist Center and his brother had set a small fire in one corner of the apartment. She asked him to leave. He wouldn't. An hour later, she found something in the crib where the baby was sleeping. A little blue teddy bear, strangled with a ribbon, a dozen straight pins stuck into its heart. The baby was unhurt, but Rae was hysterical. When she tried to breast-feed, her milk supply was low and dwindled quickly to nothing. The baby was bewildered.

Rae called Chris to come home. His brother needed that special kind of help again, she said firmly. Chris tried to talk

her out of it. The baby was screaming, wild with hunger. "He goes or we go," Rae said.

Chris sat his brother down and explained—he had to go back to the mental hospital for an evaluation, possibly for medication, just enough to get him stabilized. His brother agreed. Then he stood up, walked over to the window and put his fist through it. Chris had to wrestle him to the ground to keep him from smashing the other windows. It went on like that. It took all evening and all night for Chris to get his brother down to the psychiatric hospital in Westchester County and to get him admitted.

"Lookin' good, my man!" Norman sang as he danced around the room with the baby. Without the baby in her arms, Rae felt the full extent of her exhaustion. She moved zombie-like to the kitchen table, opened a bag of potato chips and ate one. The table was set; lunch was ready—tuna-fish salad, carrot sticks, pickles. She had done everything in advance, just in case the visit went so badly that she fell apart and forgot how to make lunch. She walked across the room and fed a potato chip to Chris.

"What would you like to drink with your lunch, Dad?" Rae asked.

"Give me Scotch."

"Iced tea, Diet Coke or Hawaiian Punch, Dad."

Norman stopped waltzing. “You’re kidding,” he said.

“Adventists don’t drink,” Rae said.

“You let her get away with that?” Norman asked Chris.

“I’m the Adventist,” he said.

“You’re not the Adventist?” Norman asked Rae. Before she could answer, he turned to Chris. “Did she get kicked out? She never wore a white blouse. Never wore *one*.”

The baby twisted away from Norman, wailing. Rae handed the bag of chips to Chris and took her son. She rose up on one toe and spun around. His wail softened to a murmur.

“What say,” Norman said, “we go out for a beer. I’d love a beer about now.”

“I told you,” Rae said to Chris. Chris put the tuna-fish salad away.

Rae and Jimmie dressed and acted like twins. They wore black. They wore their dark hair short and punk. They both had beautiful, gamine faces, though Jimmie’s eyes were more scared, Rae’s more insolent. They hooked up with Chris in New York City, sharing a flat on Avenue D. They stabilized him, he gave them direction—it was a family. The three of them were inseparable except when the men drove west on drug business. Jimmie overdosed on heroin on one of those trips. It happened in a bar somewhere in Ohio.

could ever do would make her cast him out—as long as she had a home, he had one. "Jimmie for Jimmie," she cooed to her baby. "Isn't that right, Jimmie."

Norman ordered another drink. His vitality increased. He drummed on the bar, looked around at the lingerie, tapped his foot on the bar stool. He soon ordered a third.

Chris was shaky. The fatigue was catching up with him. He leaned his back against the bar, elbows on the smooth old wood. His face looked like a Picasso—one eye seemed to hang in the cheek, the other in the forehead. Rae felt sorry. He was having a very different day than she was. The book of hope had closed on his family today. On hers, it was opening.

"Hold him," Rae said to her father, handing him Jimmie. Norman took a quick slurp of Glenlivet first. Rae walked over to Chris and sidled up between his long legs, wrapping her arms around his waist. Her touch relaxed him. He rested an arm over her shoulders. They looked at Norman.

Rae thought Norman looked a little envious of them. You could have hugged me anytime you wanted, she thought. You had sixteen years to try it. The baby writhed, then let out a scream. The pool players looked at Norman with disapproval. Norman slid off the stool and danced around the barroom floor. "No problem, Jimbo," he crowed. "You want to move, we move. You want it, you got it."

Pruitt, Ohio. That may have been the town, Chris told Rae, after looking at the map. He gave her the keys. She couldn't believe he cared enough about her to give up his keys, but he did.

Rae drove to Pruitt. She talked to the woman at the morgue, she talked to the police. There was no unidentified white male of Jimmie's height and weight logged as an OD on or about that date. In spite of that, the police captain agreed to drive Rae out to potter's field, the municipal burying grounds for unidentified bodies, usually vagrants and winos.

It was a flat field, with stubby, uninteresting grass. The captain waited on the highway in his squad car with the engine idling, the red light flashing, the two-way radio squawking. As Rae walked over the field, she commanded the soles of her feet to locate Jimmie, to tingle if they passed over him. They didn't. She gouged up a piece of the dirt anyway and dropped it into her purse.

There was a dead silence. The pool game was over, the players gone. Rae was rocking the baby in her arms.

"I lost a friend once, myself, " Norman said eventually. "Guy drove off a cliff. We'd been out on the town. Told myself I should have never let that guy get behind the wheel." He ordered another Glenlivet.

"Someone wants to die, they're going to die," Norman said. "Nothing you can do will stop them."

Rae watched Chris; his face was white. He was getting annoyed.

"Jimmie was a good-looking guy," Norman said. "But he was not a stable guy." Here came the handful of Jimmie judgments. Rae felt a surge of adrenaline. She braced herself to cut him off.

"He was well-meaning as hell," Norman said. "But bottom line: he had nothing going for him."

"Hey, man." Chris did it for her, pulling Norman's arm so that Norman had to look him in the eye. "The guy had a weak area. He didn't have to die. Do you think every man with a weak area has to die? Who would be left alive? You?"

Norman backed down. "Look," he said. "I only know what his parents told me." They were silent for a while.

"Tell more about your friend, Dad," Rae said.

"Nothing to tell."

Rae had planned to steal the van. After Ohio, she planned to go to California. Chris would never see either her or the van again. But with no body, no grave, no formality of any kind to mark the end of Jimmie, Rae couldn't go anywhere new. She

had to go back to Chris. Chris was her link—he knew and loved Jimmie as well as she did. The dirt clump in the bottom of her purse got crushed on the drive back to New York from Ohio. Over the next few weeks, it sifted slowly out of the tiny needle holes punched into the leather seams, onto the pavement of New York.

Jimmie was there in a good way at first when Chris and Rae made love, then in a bad way. Then he wasn't there at all.

Chris was going to Seventh Day Adventist meetings by then—Rae didn't know why. He was reading the Bible at night—Rae hated that. She wanted Chris to stay the same way he was when Jimmie was alive. She couldn't deal with changes—she spent most of her time sedated.

Chris spent a weekend at the retreat center upstate.

The combination of hard outdoor work and group prayer calmed and organized him. He asked Rae to move up there with him. It was a real commitment, he explained—they couldn't live together; couples had to be married. She didn't care what couples had to be as long as she had her pills. She went where Chris went—to keep Jimmie alive.

It was an Adventist ceremony, performed in their chapel by their minister. The Adventists told Rae to change out of her black sweater. She felt disloyal to Jimmie and to herself, marrying Chris in Chris's white shirt. Her vows came out sarcas-

tic. Would she honor and obey him? *Absolutely*. Would she love him? *Madly*.

For months, Rae stayed home in the attic apartment when Chris went off to work at the center. An unarticulated battle defined their days. Chris wanted her to join the center. Instead, she lay around on a bare mattress, sedated day and night. He wanted her to get the Jimmie thing behind her. He'd done it through Jesus—she could too. His voice was stern when he told her God loved her whether she liked it or not. All she had to do to be washed clean with the blood of Jesus was give up control. "Life and death are not up to you," he lectured her. "It's all up to someone bigger than you. If you'd been there when Jimmie died, you'd see that."

"If I'd been there, he wouldn't have died," Rae said.

Chris had no answer for that. Rae had watched Jimmie carefully; she monitored every drug he did. Jimmie listened to her, more often than to Chris.

Night and day, she lay on the mattress sedated, listening to tapes that reminded her of him, believing none of this had to happen.

One day, she felt the need to talk. She drove to the pancake house near the interstate, hoping to tell her sad story to any stranger who would listen. She ordered a stack of blueberry cakes with blueberry syrup, forgetting it was Jimmie's favorite

combination, the one he ordered everytime back in Seattle in the middle of the night when they were high and hungry and the pancake house was the only place open.

The stack came. She plopped on two pats of butter. She poured the blue-black syrup, bubbling with berries, over the top. When she sliced through the stack, there was a hiss, a fat, voluptuous, yeasty release of steam. It spoke to her as if it were the ghost of Jimmie.

Her drug stupor evaporated. She felt alert. She put the knife and fork down. *Jimmie?* she thought.

It's me.

How are you? she thought.

He was fine.

I have to tell you something. She was ashamed to admit it. I'm with Chris, now. He's changed completely. He's a fanatic Christian.

Jimmie knew that.

You knew? You're not jealous? You're not upset?

It's better this way.

"Not for me," she said out loud. The waitress came over to ask if she wanted something. She said no.

Better for you, Jimmie insisted. Trust me.

Rae could feel his presence weakening. Wait, she thought. I have to tell you things. I have to ask you things.

He had to go.

Love you, she thought. She left the stack uneaten and drove home. She decided to keep this a secret from Chris.

She went back to the pancake house again every day for weeks. The ghost of Jimmie did not return. She had to think of something new to do to kill time—she was bored with her tapes and quaaludes. She wandered into the home stores in the mall. For years, the pleasant items for sale in aisles like these made her feel angry. She purposely kept her living quarters harsh and blank, rebelling against the suffocating domesticity her mother had created with layers and layers, yards and yards of cloth. Her mother had not done this for her. Her mother had done it to trap her father.

Rae remembered sneaking off in a department store when she was five or six years old and peeing on a thick pile of bathroom rugs, because her mother would not take her to the bathroom. Her mother was agonizing over the color choice in satin Kleenex box covers. Rae had always distrusted and avoided cloth. Now, she revised her position. She could see how her little doll of a mother might be calmed by the sight of many erect bolts of cotton and linen, by the feeling of woven cloth rubbed between her fingers. Cloth didn't hurt anybody. It softened the edges of a hard day.

• • •

Chris had watched her as she fixed up the apartment. She bought one new thing every week or two. A tablecloth. Flowered sheets. A comforter. She could tell he was upset and dissatisfied. Something was making her happy, but how could it last if it wasn't Jesus? He tried to warn her—he told her how important it was that she take Jesus as her Savior. She smiled lovingly at him as he lectured her. She sat facing him, her arms twined around his neck. She kept the pancake house secret.

Something was making her love him, but he couldn't enjoy it. She knew he was under pressure by the Adventists to get her back to the center. They said if *his* faith was pure, *she* would come around. It was right there in Acts 16:31, "Believe in the Lord Jesus Christ and you will be saved, *you and your household*." It was tearing him apart.

One night when they were making love, he was kissing her so sweetly, she felt like she was floating. An ache of joy flowered in her. It began at the base of her spine, and spread like a bloodstain, soaking through her belly and pouring slowly upward to her heart. Everywhere she touched him, she felt her joy flow into him. He lay awake afterward, shaking. She *did*—she loved him madly.

Rae felt painful twinges in her breasts as they left Hobo's and climbed into the van. Her milk was in. She raised her sweater.

Jimmie panted with excitement at the cue, his mouth opening in a huge round O, his little arms flailing his sides, fast and firm as pistons.

"Show Dad the new park," Rae said to Chris. They drove Norman to the Town of Hart Springs Recreation Area, but he didn't feel like getting out of the van to see the small waterfall. Rae could see he was sloshed.

They drove him to the orchard where you could pick your own apples. "Take some apples back to Mom," Rae said.

"She has apples," Norman said.

They drove him to the Seventh Day Adventist Retreat Center. "This place is important to me," Chris said, driving around the dilapidated buildings and grounds. He pointed out the office, the meeting center, the health spa. He'd worked on each building, fixing, painting, installing. The Adventists had gotten it through a foreclosure. It used to be a girls' camp.

"Looks like a camp," Norman said.

"I'd like you to see the inside of the chapel," Chris said.

Norman looked at his watch. "Next time," he said.

Next time. Rae leaned forward from the backseat to observe his expression, to see if he meant it. She couldn't tell. She hoped he did. She hoped very much he wasn't just saying that. She hoped things between them could be normal.

• • •

Norman asked Chris to pull off the road. They were only half a mile from the attic apartment, but Norman couldn't wait. Chris watched him puking in the woods. Everytime he thought Norman was through, Norman bent over again. He'd had eight or nine Scotches. Rae was glad Jimmie was missing this. His eyes were closed as he chugged away on the nipple. There was finally something for him to nurse. Chris leaned against the steering wheel to watch Rae nurse. She loved the look in his eyes—he was mesmerized by the eroticism of his nursing son. Rae felt it herself, her black sweater raised up over a full white breast, black boots drawn up under her bare white thighs, the baby working his cheek muscles steadily, his little throat swallowing fast, trying to keep up with the supply. In the ecstasy of having his hunger satisfied, one hand massaged the air.

They stood in the driveway next to Norman's rental car. "Chris, you're doing a great job," Norman said, shaking hands. He turned to Rae. "Your mother said to ask if there's anything else you need."

"The things she sent were fine," Rae said.

Norman nodded at length, his eyes on the concrete. Rae understood that he was struggling with an impulse to touch

her. She made it easy for him. She raised her right arm, signaling intent to embrace. He leapt at the chance, grabbing her tight with both arms, leaving a tiny air pocket for Jimmie. It was pretty intense. Rae could see why her mother liked him. The rough feel of him contradicted his clean, Sears smell. He kissed her forehead. She detected the sour, vomitty note on his breath. She felt repelled and at the same time, greedy for more. All along, she could have used more of this. Better not to think about that.

Norman climbed in his car. He rolled down the window and reached out to wiggle the baby's foot. "Take care of Jimmie Number Two," he said and drove away.

Quinn's Wedding

Cecilia slipped the red cotton sheath over her head. She thought of it as a bright red—at home in the trailer it looked bright. Here in the fancy guest room of her father's townhouse in Lancaster, Pennsylvania, where the lighting was better, the dress was a tired red, a red that remembered being bright. The last time she'd worn it, she'd gone to a friend's funeral. At least it was tight—she was bursting out in front. She looked good. At thirty-six, she had the same little waist and good legs she'd had as a teenager, same full head of glossy black hair, same huge, dark, naughty eyes.

She leaned into the mirror, examining her face to see what makeup was needed. Not much—her eyes looked a little

tired, that was all. They'd been up since five—she and Rafael, her little boy. They'd driven straight through from Montauk, New York—eight hours in her loud, cold Volkswagen bug. Cecilia dabbed a bit of foundation over the dark circles under her eyes as Rafael watched—there was so much less to do with no bruises to cover up. She brushed black mascara on her eyelashes.

Rafael especially liked to watch her stroke on the bright, red lipstick. He held his mouth the way she held hers, lips open, stretched into a square. He looked adorable in the clip-on bow tie. Cecilia had borrowed his dress suit from her AA sponsor. The pants were too long—she had to fold the cuffs over twice, but the jacket fit.

Quinn was getting married today, but it wasn't to see Quinn that Cecilia had come speeding for eight straight hours. Cecilia hadn't even planned to come to this wedding until a week ago. Her friends convinced her she could go, she should go—in spite of anything that might happen—to see Roy-anne. Royanne, her heartbreak, raised in Florida by Sandra, Cecilia's religious sister. Royanne and her aunt had attended many more family functions than Cecilia. Cecilia hadn't attended any. Now she was ready. Her friends had been working on her. They believed she could handle this without slipping.

There was a voice at the bathroom door, female, southern. "Mama?"

"Baby!" Cecilia cried. She slipped her feet into the old black flats. The soles were thin and the arches broken. "Your sister is here," she said to Rafael. He opened the door.

Royanne stood at the threshold in a long green-lace bridesmaid's gown, dark and doe-eyed, a young version of Cecilia, but sexy in an innocent way, not an out-and-out slut like her mother. When Royanne knelt down to hug Rafael, her eyes remained on her mother. Cecilia was touched—no one had ever looked at her with such forgiveness.

"Oh baby," Cecilia said to Royanne. "Baby, baby!" They fell together in a hug that enveloped Rafael.

Royanne had gone to Jacksonville when she was four. It was Cecilia's decision. She couldn't stay off heroin; she couldn't keep her lowlife friends out of the trailer. She wanted Royanne to have a chance in life.

Rafael gathered a handful of each dress, green lace and red cotton and tugged hard, forcing the attention his way.

"Stop it," Cecilia said, looking down at him.

Rafael gave her his Latin-lover look. He was only half-Hispanic, but he had it down, sexuality mixed with divinity and ego. He wanted Royanne to himself. He jumped into her arms, legs encircling her waist.

Cecilia's children did not look related. Royanne's father was white trash. He was in jail for murder. Rafael's father was a big baby. He'd gone back to Puerto Rico to live with his mother.

Cecilia fought an urge to rush both her kids out of there, out of the house, out of town, to get them to some safer place. "Is my father around?" she asked Royanne.

"He's at the church," she said. "Organizing everything. You know how he is."

Cecilia phrased the next question carefully. "How does he treat you?" Her heart raced.

"He flirts," Royanne said. Anger brightened in Cecilia's stomach like a bed of red-hot coals. She hoped her Montauk friends were right; she hoped she was ready for this.

"Come see the dress," Royanne said. The decor throughout the townhouse was completely unlike the dark, convoluted bungalow where Cecilia, Sandra and Quinn had grown up. Their father's second wife made life sunny and practical.

The master bedroom was vast and plush, the color of wheat. Two bridesmaids, dressed in green like Royanne, had kicked off their heels and were walking back and forth in front of the mirror, looking at their reflections as they conducted a very personal conversation. Royanne gave Cecilia the stuck-up sign, lifting the tip of her nose into the air. She pulled her mother into the dressing room.

Standing before the mirrored vanity was Quinn. With her white butch haircut, frosted plum lipstick, and the diamond in her nose, Quinn looked to Cecilia like a science-fiction bride. And the dress! Cecilia wouldn't even know how to go about *wanting* a dress like that. It was made of dull ivory crepe. It fell straight from Quinn's shoulders to the floor with no ruffles, no waist. Was the word for it *chemise*?

Quinn and Sandra were disagreeing about the pearls. Quinn thought two long loops, Roaring Twenties style. Sandra thought three would be chaste, even four.

"Hi baby," Cecilia said.

Quinn screamed. She threw herself at Cecilia. They hugged for real, body up against body. Quinn knew how hard it was for Cecilia to come to her wedding.

Sandra, the maid of honor, waited out the emotional display, shifting her weight from heel to heel and swallowing a few times. Sandra looked foolish in the low-cut gown. She didn't have the body for it. She didn't have the body for anything. What she had was faith. Faith and belief, belief perfected over the years in Bible Study Group—that's what wore Sandra's clothes. She looked like a monk in drag.

Quinn turned the embrace into the rocking hug familiar to the sisters as children. "Who's my baby, who's my darling," Cecilia said to Quinn as they rocked. It was what she'd said over and over since Quinn was born; when Quinn was hyster-

ical only Cecilia could calm her down. "Who's my baby, who's my darling."

"Your dress," Sandra said to Quinn. "Look." As Sandra pulled her away, Quinn whispered to Cecilia, "I'm incredibly high."

Sandra showed Quinn her reflection in the mirror. The hug had pressed a wrinkle in the crepe, a wrinkle shaped vaguely like a soft paper airplane.

"It's pointing to my what's-it," Quinn said. "To show Jonah where to put it." She screamed with laughter. Royanne and Cecilia broke up too. Rafael's little face lit up with a precocious macho pride.

"Everybody!" Quinn called the bridesmaids into the dressing room. "This is the greatest lady in the world!" She wrapped an arm around Cecilia. They barely looked at Cecilia; they thought she was the help. "Hello, bitches," Quinn said. "This. Is my sister from New York who took care of me when our mom died."

"Oh, hi," one said.

"Hi," said the other.

Rafael was upset by the introduction. His mom, too, had almost died. He reached for his mother. She took him into her arms. He held her tight, his head in her neck. "I'm here, baby," Cecilia said to him, "I'm here."

He was the one who found her unconscious. He got off the school bus at 2:30 P.M. as usual, and ran up to the trailer. He couldn't wake her. "It's okay, baby," Cecilia said to Rafael, stroking his back and holding him tight. "I'm here."

Outside a horn honked. The limousine had arrived. The bridesmaids slipped on their green-satin high heels. They secured their matching silly pillbox hats. They gathered their purses.

Cecilia had not officially greeted Sandra yet. "Hi, Sandy," she said.

"Hi, Cece." Sandra's eyes zigzagged judgmentally over Cecilia's dress, too low, too tight—and red. Cecilia removed five twenty-dollar bills from her purse and put them in Sandra's hand. "A down payment on what I owe you." Sandra looked at the money in her hand as if there was a catch. "Are you still going to AA?"

"My one-year sobriety anniversary is tomorrow," Cecilia said. She expected Sandra to embrace her, but Sandra clasped the gold cross on the chain around her neck. "Thank you, Jesus!" she cried, raising her eyes in victory. "Thank you, thank you!"

Cecilia followed Sandra down the hall to the front door. Sandra's shoulder blades looked bony and boyish in the low-backed dress. The skin was pale and freckled. Cecilia had

tried to protect Quinn when they were little. But she'd forgotten to try to protect Sandy.

Cecilia's AA sponsor, Bonita, wasn't surprised at Cecilia's revelation. It had happened to Bonita too, with a brother, not a father. "We think we can get back at them by killing ourself," Bonita instructed. "We can't. If we survive and flourish, that's what hurts them the most." Taking Bonita's advice, Cecilia telephoned her sisters to tell them what their father had done, where he'd done it and how often. Sandra cut Cecilia off. "You're imagining things," Sandra said. "Your brain's been fried." Those were the last words spoken between them on the subject.

Quinn had let Cecilia say what she had to say, though it was hard for Cecilia to make herself heard—Quinn was in a room full of people partying to loud music.

Royanne didn't know yet. Cecilia was going to tell her this very afternoon. After the wedding, when everyone was dancing, when everyone was drunk.

Cecilia and Rafael stood in the driveway, watching the bride and her maids piling into the limousine, a white Cadillac outfitted with a bar. There was room for one more. Rafael wanted to go. It was hard for Cecilia, but she let him. She was still afraid of what she might do to herself if she was alone and feeling left out. The white Cadillac purred as it backed out of

the driveway. She climbed into the old blue bug and followed the Cadillac to the church.

The revelation had come to Cecilia at the Montauk Diner one slow afternoon a few months into her first try at AA. She was wiping up the table in the corner booth. She had just served a family of five. They made a mess. Their youngest was three. They gave him saltines. He sucked on one, then squeezed it into pulp. He opened his palm to show Cecilia—wet cracker crumbs were pressed into his fate line. The sight of his little palm opened up a hole in Cecilia's head, the hole Royanne had slipped through. Cecilia wanted a drink, bad. She wanted to kill herself. She went to the ladies' room to smoke a cigarette. Watching herself in the mirror, she inhaled extra long and hard, hoping to burn the back of her miserable throat.

Cleaning up the booth when the family was gone was a challenge. They left food everywhere. Cecilia was leaning into the table, wiping the Formica surface with the sour dishrag. The pressure of the table edge on her hipbones brought it all back. Her father used to have sex with her. He used to come into her room after she put herself to bed. His socks clicked with static as he crossed the carpeted floor. His pale-blue boxer shorts loomed before her. Sometimes she hated it.

Sometimes he stroked her hair and that felt comforting. Her mother lay in the next room dying of cancer. Cancer, that was what happened in their house. This, with her father, never happened. She was six years old.

Cecilia sat in the pew with Rafael on her lap, observing. This church was no church she'd ever been to. This church was social, recreational, streamlined. Like the townhouse. Like her father and stepmother's life together. The old church, the church where her mother's funeral was held was more sin-oriented, with dark, mottled, gouged-up pews and a heart-breaking stained glass window, Jesus forsaken in the Garden of Gethsemane.

The organ music was modern and tense. Cecilia looked at the people on the groom's side. People of quality. Quinn would have a nice life if she could get off cocaine. She had confided in Cecilia. She and her husband-to-be owed twenty-five thousand dollars. It had gone right up their noses. They hoped to use wedding gift money to get out of debt.

Cecilia tried to think of her mother. Her thoughts were vague. Her mother had been cool and self-occupied, then she got colon cancer and died. Her mother was not really a part of this family. If her mother was a spirit in heaven, smiling

down on earth this day, Cecilia guessed it was not on Quinn's wedding, but on some happy scene from her own childhood, from a time when her life was still ahead of her, and her organs were beautiful and bright like the see-through pages in the biology book at school.

Cecilia looked at her watch. It was three o'clock on the dot. Her Montauk friends were thinking of her right now. She knew exactly where they were and what clock they were looking at. Jerome was on duty in the emergency ward of the Montauk hospital. He would be looking at the big clock on the wall, the one he checked when he did intake reports. Jerome was a black nurse with huge, smart eyes, the eyes of a stag, Bambi's father. He'd fixed her up many times when she came in battered. He was also the one who got her stomach pumped. It was Jerome's idea to get Cecilia into AA. He always gave her a stern bedside talk before he let her leave the hospital. She'd given him a maroon velour sweatshirt for Christmas. This is right up my alley, he said. How'd you know? All you black guys love velour, she said.

Bonita, the AA sponsor, would be looking at her watch as she corrected work sheets at her dining-room table. Bonita taught third grade at Montauk Elementary. Until she'd gone to an AA meeting, Cecilia had no idea a nice, warm, roly-poly third-grade teacher like Bonita could be an alcoholic. In fact,

everyone in Montauk who wasn't in a bar was in AA. It was that kind of a place. Something about the sea.

And Mitchell. Sweet, flabby, weak-eyed Mitchell was tending bar in his tavern out on the Old Montauk Highway by the sea. Mitchell would be looking over his shoulder at the goofy Day-Glo bar clock, pouring himself a shot of Old Grand-Dad to toast Cecilia, whom he'd loved to distraction for fifteen years, whom he'd kept in bourbon as long as she asked him, whom he'd offered to marry whenever she came in mentally or physically destroyed by a man. "Give me a rain check, Mitch," she said every time. She wanted to marry Jerome.

All three had pushed her toward this journey. They wanted her to see Royanne as much as possible, even if seeing Royanne meant she had to see her father.

The minister came down the steps of the nave and raised his arms, signaling the audience to rise. He was dressed like a minister, in long white robes, but his manner was that of an infomercial spokesman. The organ music shifted to the processional. Down the aisle came the groom. He was cute. He had a hard prep school chin and a childish cowlick. Following the groom were his best man and three second-best men. All in white tuxes, they looked splendid, lining up on the minister's left like Top Forties crooners.

A hush fell over the wedding guests. Sandra advanced with

embarrassment, jerking forward off the beat—she had no sense of rhythm. Next came the bridesmaids, the two snobs, walking slow and with exaggerated formality like people never walk. Royanne was last, hurrying up the aisle as if to get it over with.

It looked like it was supposed to look, the beautiful ladies in gowns, the beautiful men in tuxes. It was time for Quinn to walk down the aisle. With him. Cecilia faced the back of the church. She hadn't seen her father since she was sixteen and pregnant and he'd gotten her out of jail. He told her to get out of his new life—he was planning to remarry. The organist played "Here Comes the Bride."

Standing on tiptoe, craning her neck, Cecilia saw pieces of him twice, first the torso, then the jaw above the black tie. Then he passed her with Quinn on his arm. They were walking at a normal pace, both smiling, both relaxed. They looked like they were having fun. They weren't stiff or nervous with each other. Cecilia felt betrayed. Quinn had to be high to pull this off. She knew how Quinn really felt. She was pretty sure Quinn had dismemberment fantasies.

As for her father, he looked good. He had the extra inch of fat in the chin that Cecilia had anticipated. The barrel chest had sunk to a barrel waist. His hair was white and glorious, just as it had been black and glorious. His face was still immac-

ulate, twinkling, critical, two-dimensional and utterly corrupt.

The ceremony began. Adrenaline flowed through Cecilia's veins. She felt like she could lift the church off its foundation. Who gives this woman? the minister asked. Her father said, I do. Cecilia watched him kiss Quinn on the lips. The kiss could not possibly be lasting this long. If it were lasting this long, the minister would stop him. The groom would stop him. The people in the front pew would stop him. But he seemed to know what he could get away with.

He sat down by his wife. She was a nice lady, a travel agent. The minister said a few things. Quinn and Joshua or Jonah exchanged rings. "You may kiss the bride," the minister said. The groom did not react. He was high too. Quinn gave him a big hint, pursing her frosted plum lips.

The recessional sounded and they strode down the aisle, husband and wife. In a rush of green satin and white crepe, everyone was gone—the altar was empty and boring again. The guests on both sides were smiling at each other. Cecilia was watching her father, waiting for him to notice her. He was greeting the people around him with a handshake, acknowledging those farther away with a suave twinkling of the eyes. He saw Cecilia. No reaction—after twenty years. He was masterful.

The guests exited slowly, filling the aisles. Cecilia waited for him to pass her. She saw him whisper into his wife's ear as they approached Cecilia's pew. Smoothly, he offered his wife in his stead. "This is Virginia," he said to Cecilia coolly.

"So pleased to meet you," Virginia said, her extra-warm tone compensating discreetly for her husband's distant manner with his own daughter. Virginia's chin came toward Cecilia in greeting—it could turn into a hug or a kiss depending on Cecilia's move.

Cecilia did not want to rebuff Virginia, but she wasn't going to let Old Dad call every shot.

"This is Grandpa," Cecilia said to Rafael, in a countermove, offering Rafael in her stead. They were at a standstill. Virginia's chin froze in place. Virginia wasn't Grandpa.

Sunlight streamed through the skylights of the mirrored reception hall. Cecilia liked a dark reception hall better. She liked her food dark too. This food looked like art: bright, symmetrical and intimidating. The waiters brought a new course every ten minutes. Cecilia and Rafael were sitting alone at a round table for eight. Cecilia was starting to fall apart. She tried to hide it by using unnaturally formal manners, patting her lips between bites with a linen napkin that

was still folded. Rafael slumped in his folding chair. His face was sullen—there was nothing on the whole menu he liked. He wanted cake. Cecilia twiddled the stem of her water glass. There were half-full glasses of white wine within easy reach. She didn't know if she could get through this without a drink after all. Everyone around her was having a good time. Everyone knew someone. Cecilia thought she would be seated with Royanne, but Royanne was far, far away, laughing and drinking with the guests of honor at the long table on the dais. Cecilia wished she hadn't come. She wondered if she and Raphael should go home.

The band began to play Quinn and Jonah's song. Instead of going down to the dance floor, they slow-danced lazily on the dais for a few measures, then sat down again, Quinn on Jonah's lap. Cecilia's father didn't like that. He took over. He pulled Quinn up and led her to the varnished floor. Smooth and agile in front of all the wedding guests, he danced with the bride. Too close. The song was "Time after Time."

After dancing too close with Quinn, her father danced too close with Sandra. Sandra looked terrified. She danced horribly, stepping out of her father's embrace when she wasn't supposed to, only to be slammed too close on the next beat. He went for one of the blond bridesmaids next.

Rafael asked Cecilia to take him to the bathroom. As she

led him out down the hall, something bothered her, something nagged at her not to leave the ballroom. She pushed open the swinging door that read MEN. The men's room was vast, upsetting her. She followed Rafael inside. He was astonished by the richness of the room, so astonished he peed on the wall and the floor, looking around at the marble stalls, up at the crystal chandelier. She was glad he soiled the room—it deserved to be soiled. It was too rich. He washed his hands. Then, neither one could find the door. There were too many mirrors. No one was there to help when she needed it most.

Finally Rafael found the exit. She grabbed his hand and ran with him down the hall to the great sunny room. Her father was dancing with Royanne, close, very close, front to front. The song was "On the Street Where You Live." Royanne looked trapped and embarrassed. Anger again brightened in Cecilia's stomach like red-hot coals.

"Sit, baby," Cecilia said to Rafael, pointing to his chair. "And stay sat." She crossed the room to the dance floor. In front of all those decent and intimidating people, she approached her father from behind. She couldn't believe she was doing this without the help of booze or drugs. She tapped him on the shoulder.

He smiled. He thought she was cutting in, replacing Royanne, but she was replacing him. She slid in front of him, gath-

ered her daughter into dance position, and waltzed away. He looked foolish, rooted to the spot on the dance floor where Cecilia had tricked him, arms raised to embrace a partner, grasping thin air.

When he recovered, he went for Royanne again, gliding across the varnished oak, arms raised for the target. Cecilia dodged him, ducking and yanking Royanne out of his reach. Again he stood, baffled, empty-handed. The bass player laughed.

Cecilia's father shifted into his belligerent mode. He went straight for Cecilia and grabbed her wrist hard, prying her fingers away from Royanne's. The wedding guests began to pay attention. It was getting scary—Cecilia didn't know if she could pull this off. "Go, Roy," she said. "Get away from him." But Royanne stayed. Royanne pried her grandfather's fingers away from Cecilia's wrist. Up on the dais, Quinn screamed. Cecilia gave her father a look: *Back off*. She and Royanne danced away down the floor.

He made his face blank. You don't exist, it said. Again Quinn screamed. He wiped his forehead with a handkerchief and stood off to one side, patting his cummerbund and smiling out at the guests as if everything he'd planned and paid for was just as it should be. The pace was slowing, the song was ending, Quinn was screaming. Cecilia lowered Royanne in a graceful, theatrical close.

As an acknowledgment to Cecilia, the bass player played the raunchy Rolling Stones bass line to "Honky Tonk Women." Instead of leaving it at that, the other players tore into the song, one that was slated for much, much later in the afternoon, when the old fogies were sobering up with coffee and the young people had taken over the dance floor.

Cecilia could never hear that song without dancing. She got her shoulders going, she swung her pelvis easy and low. Royanne danced beside her mother, showing off her own hot moves. Hers were a generation newer, like the ones the lady rappers did on MTV.

Quinn was holding her white butch head with both hands, yelling out the chorus with the band.

The guitarist launched into the second verse. Cecilia rocked her hips, she stroked her thighs in her tight red dress—what else was a tight red dress for? She raised her arms high over her head. Royanne moved about her mother in a circle, all profile and smooth as liquid mercury, Egyptianesque. Rafael could obey no longer. He jumped down out of his chair and ran up to join his family. Angelic and precociously male, he mamboed effortlessly across the wide floor.

Thanksgiving with Dorrie & Heck

Willa's whole body is keening toward some ominous revelation. A detail somewhere in the decor wishes to speak to her privately. Her eyes scan all surfaces, the nubby sofa, the cracked black leather of the lopsided Eames chair, the lonely Mexican blanket over the mantle. This is her brother's home, but it's not his taste. It's all Dorrie, Dorrie the unsteady, sentimental genius. It's Thanksgiving again; again the two families are celebrating; again between Dorrie's huge, average turkey dinner and Willa's showy selection of pies, there's talent, too much talent, and it's too important: the children perform (both Willa and her brother have seventeen-year-old sons and fifteen-year-old daughters) and Willa's children lose. Only Willa wins; she wins at pies.

The pies are in the oven warming, apple, mince and pumpkin with sugar-sprinkled lattice crusts, pastry cutouts of birds and ivy, a meringue stacked high as a *Playboy* centerfold. The kids' performances are now under way. Willa leans in the kitchen doorway as her son, Charles, begins to juggle; she wants to be near the pies, to pull them out of the oven the moment she hears one sizzle or pop.

Her gaze falls on Wade. The coarse, pale-blue W tattoo on the back of her husband's right hand is growing vaguer with the years. Wade used to be rough around the edges; now he's subtle. The undiscriminating enthusiasm of his blue eyes for example, has tempered to a precise and elegant fire. His clothes used to precede him into a room; now they're disciples: the dove-gray cashmere V neck, the skinny Levis lie against him with spiritual candor: they've found bliss. It's unfair. In eighteen years, Willa's gone from stunning to average, just as Wade has gone from average to stunning. Willa's Brigitte Bardot pout and body have disappeared. She's blurred, she's bland, she crowds every inch of a size 12.

Her nephew, Jordan, is up next. He demonstrates an original theorem. Jordan got into MIT, Early Admissions. All ten of the colleges Willa's son is considering are "safe schools." Dorrie and Heck's kids are lean and precocious in the hard-drive, high-IQ way. Willa and Wade's kids are beautiful and

popular. Willa and Wade have much, much more money than Dorrie and Heck.

Their youngest is sitting in Wade's lap, astride his leg. Jill, the symmetry-breaker Jill, the five-year-old thread from which Willa's marriage dangles. Both Wade's arms are around Jill's waist. His chin nestles in the crown of her soft brown curls. Willa wants to take a snapshot. Their family photograph album is filled with pictures exactly like this: Wade with Jill, Wade with Clae, Wade with Charles. Willa is always out of the picture. She likes to keep a distance of twelve to fifteen feet between Wade and herself at all times. At home this morning, Wade approached her from behind as she fussed with a lattice crust, and he placed his palm affectionately around the back of her neck. She pretended to be too busy to notice his touch and stepped forward out of his grasp, but really she was rejecting him.

Wade was up from the ranks. He drove a food-service delivery route before Willa's father handpicked him to join the sales staff of the shoe company. Willa's brother wanted no part of shoe biz as he called it—he was completing a Ph.D. in Physics. Willa's father bought Wade his first suit and tie; he took Wade for his first good haircut. He sent Wade out on the road. And just as Willa's father predicted, Wade did well. He's hungry, her father said. In this business you've got to be hun-

gry. In every encounter, in every transaction, you've got to want to win. And Wade won Willa.

Now Willa's older daughter is playing the saxophone. Clae is sexy in her black high-top sneakers and pink socks, her skinny black sheath and Brigitte II pout, but the song she plays, "Take Five," is leaden, a whale on Valium. Willa feels keen. Something is about to be revealed, something is about to be explained. She listens hard to the breathing of everyone present, she scans their faces for clues: warm, hot, hotter, cold.

Six years ago, Wade fell in love with Karen Summerhouse, the twenty-nine-year-old saleswoman under him at the office who won Top Regional Producer. Willa knew, she felt it happening, it was as obvious as if Wade had laid an egg for her. First, he despised Karen Summerhouse, then he accepted Karen Summerhouse, then he praised Karen Summerhouse, then he created a special award for Karen Summerhouse, then he stopped talking about Karen Summerhouse for a year. He did a lot of errands. He did them in the most annoying, painful way, walking around the house with his hands in his pockets, his eyes on the misty, sweaty ecstasies of the near future. He always said he was going to the store.

One afternoon, Wade came to Willa, yawning and stretching, trying to appear incapable of loving anyone or anything.

He was thinking of moving out for a while, he said. He just wanted a change.

"Who have you told about this?" she said.

"No one," he said. They both meant her father.

"Good," she said. "Because I'm pregnant." Wade flinched. "Don't make a face," she said. "I have no qualms about getting rid of it." She believed in abortion. So did her father. Wade did not. "It's not a problem," she said. "It's no different than leaving a house in a flood."

"A house with someone still in it," he said. He turned his back to her, the hand with the blue tattoo rubbing the back of his neck across the hairline. When Wade was first selling shoes in other cities, he spent hours on the road. To follow his progress emotionally, Willa would think of the blue W winding its way across Louisiana, Texas, New Mexico. She regretted that psychic connection now.

While Wade rubbed the back of his neck, trying to decide, Willa refolded her undies. Later when she opened the bureau drawer and saw them, she screamed—she'd folded each one into a tight, tiny packet the size of a matchbook and stacked them next to his. He stayed.

For two years, there was a point during every dinner party when Wade began to praise Karen Summerhouse. Here she was, born dirt-poor, yet Karen Summerhouse was sheer class.

She could sweep into a buyer's office in a navy-blue Ungaro and get him to sign for double the order he had in mind without even knowing what hit him. Yet Karen was aware of her roots—she could shoot, skin and dress a deer and did in fact take a week off every November to do just that.

Willa was afraid their friends would notice the unfortunate regularity of the watertight Karen Summerhouse speech. To disguise the fact that her heart was breaking, Willa began to chime in appropriately, saying, "She approaches life with no conceptual limits," after the words *sheer class*, or perhaps, "This is amazing," right before Wade got to the sentence about the deer.

During this period Willa caught Wade looking at his watch while they were hugging. She picked up the phone at 1 A.M.—they had separate bedrooms by now—and heard his voice, intimate and confiding, describing his day.

Willa's niece, Anita, sits down at the upright. She plays "The Moonlight Sonata" with a cold, bright proficiency, passionless as a compact disc. The chords flow fast and loud from her fingertips; even her pinkie reaches the proper key every time, inhumanly accurate. Willa listens hard, but to the walls, to the pauses between heartbeats, not to Anita.

Lined up on display in the sideboard behind Wade, Dorrie's angel collection makes a heavy case against heaven. There are

simply too many angels in a row. Instead of producing a celestial air, they exude the cold worminess of an old Italian-American cemetery. Every day for seven days after Wade announced he was staying, Willa contemplated aborting Jill just to spite him. And now there they sit, father and daughter.

Willa did not know why Wade stopped seeing Karen but she knew when. Suddenly there was more of him at home when he was home. Suddenly he needed her approval again.

The pies are warm. Willa removes them silently as Anita brings Beethoven to a flawless, high-velocity finish. Anita lowers her fingers into the final chord, holding the keys rock solid still, emoting into them as if she is changing the sound even as it rises into the living-room air. Heck starts the applause. Dorrie lights a cigarette.

Anita seats herself on the sagging sofa next to her mother. She picks up her mother's free hand and examines the recent manicure. Dorrie, who almost discovered a vitamin in the research lab at Einstein (it turned out to be something else—Willa forgets what) is smoking instead of clapping. Everyone knows she's heartbroken, she's thinking of her mother, a concert pianist who died in a freak accident in Mexico. That's it. That is the revelation. Willa's riveted by the vignette: she vows to try Dorrie's way, to reveal her breaking heart instead of passing her torture off as fun even as the rack is turning. Let

the chips fall where they may. Let there be—she's thinking of Anita—human sacrifice.

Willa applauds louder to make up for Dorrie. She's glad the competition is over for another year. But Jill is sliding off her father's lap, Jill is approaching the "stage." This was not planned. Clae moves in, standing behind Wade, draping both bangle-ridden arms around his neck, resting her cheek against his. Wade is at home with her touch, doesn't even notice that one daughter or the other is always beside, behind, on top of him. It's a familiar sight, Clae and Wade cheek-to-cheek—it's the way they read the paper, the way they watch the evening news, yet Willa is seeing it for the first time for what it is. I subconsciously assigned my daughters to do that, she thinks, to sit on him, to hold him down because I am ashamed that I no longer have the appeal to. This is a second revelation. Willa had assumed there would only be one.

Jill spends two minutes carefully arranging her skirt. Her plaid wool dirndl is forest green, her white sailor blouse is embroidered with ducks. Green grosgrain ribbons loop lazily in her soft brown hair. She looks like the perfect five-year-old until she opens her mouth to sing, then she looks like a tiny transvestite from the Florida Panhandle where Wade was born. *Goodbye, Joe, me gotta go, me oh my oh, Me gotta go pole the pirogue down the bayou.*

Jill's loud, heart-wrenching country voice with its preco-

cious edge of desperation is campy and creepy. It's all there by osmosis: Wade's childhood on the Panhandle, the salt of the Gulf of Mexico hanging in the air, eroding the bodies of trucks, eroding the minds of the locals, making the coastal community so sleepy, so heavy it would be no surprise if the border dissolved completely, sending the whole state drifting southward into the tropics where it belongs.

My Yvonne, the sweetest one, me oh my oh, Son of a gun, We'll have big fun on the bayou.

Clae mouths the phrases in unison with Jill, swaying to the beat with her arms around Wade's neck, so his entire upper body sways with her. Every corner of Wade's face is crinkled up and pink with pride. Everyone in the family has heard Jill sing this song; no one knew she was planning to join the talent show this year.

Jambalaya and a crawfish pie and a fillet gumbo, 'Cause tonight I'm gonna see my cher a mio.

Jill attacks the notes with the precision of a tiny bird, ending each phrase with a sexy hiccup or a complex trill. After the second chorus, Heck starts to applaud prematurely. Jill angrily shakes her head no and without missing a beat, launches into the third verse.

Settle down far from town, get me a pirogue, Swap my mon to buy Yvonne what she need-o.

Dorrie is grinning her wonderful raggedy grin as if to say,

the kid's got it! Anita's face is wounded with each gram of attention her mother freely gives. Wade and Clae sway as one. In a crazy, head-to-toe moment of breathless, organized foolishness, Willa finds herself crossing the room, lifting Clae's arms away from Wade, replacing them with her own. If she no longer has the power to hold him, she wants everyone to know. Let him rise out of his seat and float away to a new life in a condo with a twenty-nine-year-old woman if not this very minute, then after dessert or by noon tomorrow.

Wade does a double take, looking up over his shoulder at Willa, shocked, trapped, ashamed, chastened, lonely, grateful, forgiven, pleased. He covers her arms with his; on top is the hand with the blue W. Wade's touch, the heat of his palm, the tension of his grasp.

Pick guitar, fill fruit jar and be gay-o, Son of a gun, we'll have big fun—Jill holds *gun*, then *fun* longer than any pair of five-year-old lungs should be able to do, so long the room erupts with clapping and raucous hoots, all those present are aching for her to end the song.

On the bayou.

Willa tries to loosen her hands to join in the applause, but Wade won't let her. He holds on tight, tighter than ever. Restrained by Wade, Willa feels desire. Her body heats up in a slow sequential capitulation from the back of her neck to the

arches of her feet. Desire, the lying diplomat, the underhanded snitch, is visiting her territory by territory, giving her back to Wade for nothing. Clae rolls her eyes at her parents: she strongly disapproves of their unnatural public display. She blocks them from sight as she jumps up and down, whooping for Jill.

After the applause dies down, the amazing pies are sliced and eaten, Clae and her uncle sneak out for a smoke, then Heck trounces Wade at chess (Wade gets better every year, but he's still not good enough to win). The boys retire to throw shuriken darts at Jordan's Partridge Family poster/target. Jordan skillfully misses and catches Charles in the neck half an inch from an artery. Things have turned too Mayan. Willa tells off Heck: This is the last Thanksgiving we spend with you. In the emergency waiting room, Wade reaches for Willa's hand. When they are home and alone at last, he reaches for everything.

They are falling asleep when she hears the cat crying at the back door. She walks through the house barefoot in the dark and lets the cat in. She leans in the open doorway, hugging her arms, fascinated by the night. The wind licks elegantly at the bare branches of the giant sycamore tree. A hard winter dew shines on the strong, still-green grass. There's a hum, a chord —the hymn of nature. Everything is stunning and alive.